BUBU OF MONTPARNASSE

BUBU

OF MONTPARNASSE

BY

CHARLES-LOUIS PHILIPPE

TURTLE POINT

TRANSLATED FROM THE FRENCH
BY LAURENCE VAIL

INTRODUCTION

SINCE his death, aged thirty-five, in 1909, Charles-Louis Philippe has become the object of something like a cult. A minor novelist, certainly, or rather a novelist exploring a narrow seam, he is now recognized as one of the most individual, as well as influential, of modern French writers. His letters, journals and novels, which, apart from *Bubu*, include *La Mère et l'Enfant*, *Père Perdrix*, *Marie Donadieu*, and *Charles Blanchard*, have established him both as an artist of quite remarkable purity and as a fore-runner of the social-realism that became popular in England and Germany during the thirties. A peasant by birth, his writing has some of the sturdiness, the painstaking realism reinforced by strange lyrical undertones, of a painting by the Douanier Rousseau. Less arrestingly bizarre than Rousseau, however, Philippe is also a much more self-conscious artist—a writer acutely aware of the social structure, of his own place in it, and yet never a propagandist at the expense of being a craftsman. His novels, of which *Bubu de Montparnasse* is usually regarded as the greatest, make their effects scrupulously. Their flavour, slightly dry with the strength of a good *vin du pays*, comes from the working of a taut, nervous sensibility on the problems of poor country people and of lonely provincials in big cities. Philippe, however, deals with his workmen, pimps, poor students and prostitutes, not as a *bourgeois* with his collar off, but as one who had to live within the same parallels. Yet his range is far greater than that of most proletarian writers. His novels acquire a vivid reality of their own because Philippe recreates his various kinds of life in a new, exciting context. And more than that, he is capable, in *Marie Donadieu* and

La Mère et l'Enfant especially, of suggesting the French countryside with the fresh sensuousness of Renoir, of also giving to his urban characters a sense of being part of the same historical and economic process whose background, as much as the hot, stale streets of blighted city suburbs, is the drowsy landscape of France, its rivers dawdling under blue skies, its lovers lying on banks of startling green. Philippe's women and men, sinning and corrupt as they are, follow only natural laws. They sin with a curious kind of innocence and dignity; they are old and wise in their youth with inherited experience. They try to better their conditions in order to remove the barriers that exist between them and the rich. In their sufferings they have the hurt pathos of wounded animals, and because they are always real people, they never appear within their frames posed with the stiff awkwardness common to the photographs of their day.

Philippe, though much admired by a small fashionable circle, never reached a great public in his lifetime. But each year that passes sees his formal place in the hierarchy of French literature grow more secure, and his legend increase. When, in 1932, *Bubu* appeared in a limited edition in Paris, T. S. Eliot wrote in a Preface: 'The book has always been for me, not merely the best of Charles-Louis Philippe's books, but a symbol of the Paris of that time . . . In a very much smaller way, *Bubu* stood for Paris as some of Dickens's novels stand for London . . . Philippe had a gift which is rare enough: the ability not to think, not to generalize. To be able to select, out of personal experience, what is really significant, to be able not to corrupt it by afterthoughts, is as rare as imaginative invention . . . He is saying what he has to say, not writing a book.'

Philippe's biography, published in 1942 under the title of *Charles-Louis Philippe, Mon Ami*, by Émile Guillaumin, gives a fascinating account of his life. Guillaumin, president of a group called *Les Amis de Charles-Louis Philippe*, with members of every class and race and an annual bulletin devoted to critical studies of Philippe, provides the biographical basis necessary for an understanding of his work, and for the English reader, unfamiliar generally with both Philippe's name and novels, some facts from it may be of interest.

Charles-Louis Philippe was born at Cérilly, in the *département* of Allier, in 1874. 'I was born, one August evening, in a small town that was white, grey and blue. I was born in quite a small house, rue de la Croix Blanche, made of greyish limestone and pink plaster.'

He was one of twins; his father made wooden shoes, his mother mended chairs. His parents, his relationship with whom he describes touchingly in *La Mère et l'Enfant*, were poor and his own childhood was scarred by a bone disease which, as well as necessitating several operations, left its permanent mark on his face. 'An infamous mark,' he described it later. He was a slight, sensitive child, tortured by his appearance and poor physique, but delighting in the countryside, above all in country fairs. To inanimate objects he gave the devotion due to the companions of his own age, who, for a long time, he lacked. 'Wooden horses, lotteries, inns full of people, that's what gives me a feeling of life. Wooden horses are a taste of the wonders of paradise. I spend all my pocket money on them and when it's gone, I watch them going round and I give them my heart.'

Nevertheless, the physical inferiority, the loneliness of his early years, were compensated for, to some extent, by success at school. When he was twelve, he won a scholarship to the *lycée* at Montluçon, and he remained there for eight years. During this period, often alone but absorbed, the workman's child drew steadily away from the interests of his class; in the library of the local doctor, Charles Demahis, he read Voltaire and Helvetius, he grew to admire Leconte de Lisle, Hérédia, Baudelaire, Banville and Catulle Mendès. Determined to be a writer he left the *lycée* and, with some half-promises of jobs, set out for Paris. Four months later, half-starved and penniless, he was back at Cérilly. What Guillaumin calls 'the calvary of the year before' began again: the steady hunt for work, the disappointments and loneliness and frustration of life in a country labourer's cottage, when his mind had already charted its routes along the map of the imagination.

This bitter period, nevertheless, moulded him as a writer: 'I abandoned all my superior dreams, those that swaggered and those that dreamed of rich and idle occupations. . Those who work to earn their daily bread surround me and they live by the law that demands one should earn one's bread by the sweat of one's brow. I, too, am a man of the people and I want to work with them . . .'

Inaccurate, in fact, as this was, for Philippe, despite his origins, was never anything of the manual labourer, this early defeat established him in his right context. It gave him back his own identity and a natural sympathy for the poor, so that, later on, when life gave him the raw materials of his books, it went some way to writing them for him.

At the end of a year he was back in Paris with a job in the Pharmacie Centrale. He took a room in the same hotel, rue St. Dominique, where he had stayed before. He relived his ambitions, he rethought the kind of writing he wanted to do: 'Let us steep ourselves in the working-classes, live their life as closely as we can, and, understanding their wants, be their weapons.

'Art must increase its territories . . . make use of science . . . we need great clarity, an accent sharp and final as the sound of the guillotine . . .'

But his life was still hard, he was lonely, and his office work bored him. He began to long for the fresh air and solicitude of Cérilly, and he had moments of creative despair. 'I'm sick to death of literature,' he wrote with a Rimbaud-like ferocity. 'I should like to live the rest of my life in my small provincial town. I'm sick of women, I hate them. I wish Paris never existed.'

There were, however, other causes for his wretchedness. A septic gland, which had eventually to be cut, laid him low for several months and for longer than that it had been poisoning him. Now, in enforced convalescence, he began his novel *La Mère et l'Enfant*. 'It will be the story of my mother. It will show me as a child, the countryside of my youth and my home.'

Meanwhile, returning to Paris, the episode which was to result in *Bubu de Montparnasse* took place. Philippe, with few alterations of detail, has told, in this novel, a true story. To all intents and purposes he is himself Pierre Hardy. On 15 July, in the Boulevard de Sébastopol, he met, as he describes it in the novel, Maria, 'the most exquisite little creature in the world, very kind, very intelligent, very sweet and very much corrupted,' the Berthe of *Bubu*. For the first time in his life his longing for love and companionship was realized. Six weeks later Maria had to go to hospital. Six months went by and her symptoms were diagnosed as syphilis. From then on, the story faithfully conforms to the plot of *Bubu*.

Philippe had now moved to the Ile St.-Louis and, working

opposite a portrait by Leonardo and a Grünewald Christ, he finished *La Mère et l'Enfant*.

This was published in 1899. It was praised in experimental reviews for its lyrical quality, its sadness, its bitter-sweet flavour, its purity of form. By the autumn he was hard at work on *Bubu*. The novel had already been lived, it was simply a question of re-creating it as a work of art.

To this he devoted the next nine months. He wrote with passion and rewrote with the care and scrupulousness of the traditional craftsman. His life acquired new perspectives, a kind of excited, anxious happiness. He wrote to his parents that he was growing a beard: 'It is much more luxuriant than I should ever have imagined and I think I shall keep it. With it I may become a handsome young man, who will be a credit to his family.'

Maria had been replaced by a blonde young girl from Lyons. Philippe thought himself madly in love. Yet he could still write: 'There were moments when I enjoyed my solitude like a triumph.' He was now correcting proofs of *Bubu*, embarking on *Père Perdrix*, answering the large number of letters that *La Mère et l'Enfant* had brought him, all this in addition to his everyday job and the exhaustions of his love-affair. This water-tight world was roughly broken into by the reappearance of Maria. Philippe had not seen her for two years. Now, tired of being ill-treated by her procurer, determined to get away from her street-life, she wanted to take up her old work as a florist. Philippe, with the help of his friends, got together enough money to send her to Marseilles, where she said she had connections. They all saw her off at the station. News, however, filtered through at varying intervals that she had failed to find work and as she spoke in one of her rare letters of moving to Toulon 'where naval officers were numerous', it seemed that her salvation was only temporary.

Bubu had a startling success. Barrès wrote to him, also the young and famous Comtesse de Noailles. He met Gide and Francis Jammes and both friendships developed. Two women, Marguerite Audoux and Mme Mackenty, widow of an Irish Colonel, came into his life and remained loyal and devoted friends till his death. To Mme Mackenty he described his new project, *Marie Donadieu*: 'It will be a love story, with a woman who is deceitful from head to foot, generous, libelled, oppressed, nervous, sentimental, rejected by the world, thrown out of men's hearts because of the lies with which she surrounds herself.'

These qualities, so expansively listed, Philippe had applied earlier to his blonde from Lyons, shortly after the end of their affair. They are qualities applicable to most of the young women in his books, the result of the fatal attraction so common in life, leading men and women repeatedly to personalities of the same type, awakening in them the same characteristics, burning and devouring them with the same pattern of flame and ashes.

Philippe was now reading with pleasure Claudel's *L'Arbre*, Hardy's *Jude the Obscure*, Defoe's *Moll Flanders*. He admired greatly Rodin's sculpture. And he began to formulate his own ideas about contemporary literature. 'Writing must be a confession, the very expression of the writer's life . . . I find it extraordinary that the novel is being made the pretext for social and psychological studies . . . What is important is the creation of living characters . . . the real novelist puts himself in the midst of his characters, he works from the centre outwards . . . I do not believe a writer has to have education . . . For myself, if you want to know my most urgent feeling, it is this: I have a sense of class. The writers who have preceded me are all of the *bourgeoisie*. The things that interest me are not theirs . . . I find my soul in the people who surround me. I do not divide people into races but into classes . . . ordinary working people are going to be able to enter literature which in turn will be transformed by this new element . . . of course, when we think of Balzac, or Dante, or Claudel, we are beyond any kind of class distinction, for what they represent, what they have translated, is the very essence of the human spirit.'

These remarks of Philippe's are basic to an appreciation of his work. They are historically important and they give a clue to his great vogue in France during the 1920's and in Germany a decade later. Philippe was not, however, a revolutionary by political conviction, for he hated all politics and politicians, and he subscribed to no political programme. His friend Marcel Ray, in the special number of the *Nouvelle Revue Française* devoted to Philippe's work, sets his ideas in their real perspective: 'There was no need for him to go to the people, he was already of them . . . I know he was very sincerely a socialist, but he was one more by birth than doctrine. He had never read Karl Marx nor Proudhon . . . he was a socialist just as negroes are frizzy-haired: socialism was for him the feeling of a difference.'

In 1904 *Marie Donadieu* was published and narrowly missed the Prix Goncourt, awarded to Leon Frapié for *La Maternelle*. Philippe was now established as a writer and although he kept on at his office work he also lived in part the life of a professional man of letters. In 1907, when he was at work on *Charles Blanchard*, his father died. Philippe's feeling for his family, always strong, deepened. He wrote continually to his mother about his memories of his father, 'his life is an example to me'; his attachment to the past and to the country of his childhood tightened. He worked even harder, feeling himself at the height of his powers, on the threshold of new discoveries.

These were, however, not to be revealed. An attack at Cérilly of what was first regarded as influenza, then a mild typhoid, was diagnosed as meningitis. Within a week, on 21 December 1909, he was dead. His last words were 'How beautiful it is . . . dear God, how beautiful.' Gignoux, Copeau and Gide hurried from Paris, and Gide noted in his journal that Philippe's mother was very proud of them, 'the friends from Paris', and showing them her house and Philippe's own room, where he lay, said: 'We may be poor people, but you can see that we are not poverty-stricken.'

More than most novelists Philippe was able to bring the instincts behind his writing to the surface, so that his ex-pressed ideas about novel writing not only give an idea of the tangled depths concealed by the smooth exterior of his books, but are accurate about their effect. As Eliot pointed out, he realized his intentions perfectly, he was faithful to his gifts.

These gifts he used to irradiate two worlds: the provincial poor of the Bourbonnais countryside, and the Paris of those who live precariously on the margin. *La Mère et l'Enfant* recaptured, in nostalgic terms, the mingled magic and misery of the first; *Bubu de Montparnasse* his personal experience of the second. In *Marie Donadieu* he related the two, fusing the two themes of his work into a single identity.

This is not the place to discuss Philippe as a novelist and *Bubu*, in any case, is here to be read. It is enough to say that ultimately a writer survives by the seriousness he brings to his work as an artist, to the quality, in its most general sense, of his style. And Philippe, apart from his compassion, from his gifts of identification, his vividness in creating character, deserves to survive for the purity of his craftsmanship. His books have often a harsh realism, a tragic intensity, a grim detail; yet, because of the remarkable accuracy of Philippe's prose, the supple strength and economy of his narrative style, reinforced at moments by arresting images and evened out in emotional crises by drily ironic observations, the novels neither depress nor seem to exploit their squalor. Philippe has been compared, with account of his limited scope, to Dostoievsky, Dickens, and Léon Bloy. They are not deceptive comparisons. Anyone reading Philippe's books cannot fail to be struck by the revealing detail, the unsentimental characterization, the expression of a level of meaning, beauty and achievement beyond the characters' normal state of degradation but implicit in their unselfconscious behaviour, that is to be found, with varying effect, in the work of the other three. Philippe's characters are what they are because they have only the instinctive routes of their own personalities to follow. They are not equipped with much conscience, but with unsophisticated, often sentimental, impulses. They learn the hard way to live and they have to compete without moral inhibition to survive. They will never change, for change is not in their natures. But Philippe, by presenting them dispassionately in their human context, offers them the redemption open to all who are truly alive.

ALAN ROSS

PART I

CHAPTER I

BOULEVARD Sébastopol, the evening after the Fourteenth of July, was still lively. It was half past nine. The arc-lights, garishly white among the rows of trees, threw out a shadow here and there or were lost to sight in the leaves. The shops were closed: *Pygmalion*, the *Petits Agneaux*, the *Cour batave*, the *Meilleur Marché du Monde*, and, at the base of the great black buildings, their gloomy façades now seemed to darken the pavements which they had illuminated so brilliantly a short time before. The high gilded sign-boards which had gleamed in the sun on the balconies of the first, second, and upper storeys, now withdrew with their letters of yellow wood into the blackness as if, like wholesale trade, they, too, had to rest at night. Flowers and feathers, food-stuffs, fabrics, sales, had all closed their blinds and were silent along the Boulevard Sébastopol.

It was the hour when passers-by no longer pause before shop windows. Night, with other objectives, had come to life. There were lanterns on the carriages: the cabs with bright lights shining like two gloating eyes, and the trams with red or green beacons, roaring like an impatient crowd. They followed one another, crossed, stamped and rolled on. On the horizon, in the direction of the Grands Boulevards, the light was far brighter and rose into the sky as though drawn by some luminous power. At this hour, the Boulevard Sébastopol, with its closed shops, was no longer the goal. Cabs rushed by. Those bound for the Grands Boulevards went towards the light, hastening there like people attracted by a show.

The whole of the Boulevard Sébastopol lives on the pavement. On this broad area, in the blue air of a summer night, the day after the Fourteenth of July, Paris sifts and trails the residue of the holiday. The arc-lights, the trees' foliage, the moving vehicles, the diverse excitement of the passers-by, create something dense and sharp, an atmosphere both alcoholic and tired. A nightly spectacle, and yet many a façade and street-corner retains a reminder of the day before. Certain noises, certain cries recall the songs of last night's revellers. A few flags and lanterns hang at windows and seem to clamour for a renewal of festivity. One can guess what is taking place in people's minds. Those who enjoyed themselves yesterday are on the alert for some new delight. This is because men who have once known pleasure seek it eternally. While the others, those who are poor, those who are ugly, and those who are shy, make their way through the remains of the holiday and nose in the corners for some debris of pleasure that has been overlooked. This is because men who have never known pleasure are in torment and seek for it day after day until they grow weary of never having had anything at all.

The air seemed to vibrate about them. Spruce young men passed by in groups of two and three, and went their way. They wore stiff new collars, elegant and sober ties pierced with gaudy tie-pins, and they hastened off, with money in their pockets, towards the light. Shop clerks chatted together: 'We danced till midnight. She was willing enough. I took her to a hotel in the rue Quincampoix. She was just dying for it!' Two men followed in the footsteps of two little misses. Accosted, the girls looked at each other and broke into laughter. Young men with phosphorescent eyes ogled the woman when a couple passed. Fat men smoked their cigars complacently and reflected: 'I'm an important official who makes twelve thousand francs a year.' Couples passed: a smart young woman on the arm of a smart young man, she happy because she looked prosperous, he delighted because men envied him: a young girl, less smart, her sweet-heart talking to her with his thoughts on love. Other couples: a husband and wife, each looking their own way, exchanging a word now and again, their minds and bodies accustomed to each other.

They passed. Once they had passed, others came. Shop-keepers strolled by, taking as much space in the street as their own shop-windows. A young man clinging desperately to a woman's arm, slavishly following where she led. You felt he would have followed her to the world's end. Vanity, gaiety, lust walked among the lights. The air was charged with their heat. What did yesterday's fatigue matter? Warm gusts rose from the memories of the past orgy, and hearts contracted with desire. Paris seemed like a weary dog, still chasing a bitch in heat.

Whores went about their business. There was little Gabrielle who had lived two years with Robert, the man who murdered Constance. Her lover had just left her for penal servitude. And there, little Jeanne who must have been all of seventeen. She had been walking the Boulevard Sébastopol since the month before. Only a touch of powder on her cheeks, and in her eyes shone the first flames of pleasure. Many would not have taken her for a prostitute. Here were the street-walkers, some with hats, some bare-headed. Some with a heavy cow-like gait, accosting men boldly. Others swinging their hips and picking up their prey with a sly glance as they prepared their smiles. There was a group of them at the corner of the rue Rambuteau. To the left, you caught a glimpse of the dank Halles, and you thought of old stumps of cabbage. All of them chatter-ing, at the same time. Like frogs croaking near a swamp.

The vice inspectors travel in pairs. They are easy to recognize by their expression, their slovenly get-up, and their ponderous step. They are slovenly like their profession.

They walk stiffly, like people performing a public duty. They look the women up and down with a weighty stare. The stare of the passer-by merely stares, but the stare of these plain-clothes men inspects. One of them, a stout dark fellow, decorated with the *Médaille Militaire*, his coarse mug accentuated by his moustache, walks by carrying his fists like weights. Stiffly, the tarts go by, without turning their heads, well aware in their slavish minds that might is always right.

The brag and bluff of the pedlars. Whenever a policeman turns his back, up springs a pedlar. Cap on head, features twisted with animation, faded moustache, they talk excitedly, for their passions are violent and they must earn enough to eat and drink. Here's one of them, not yet eighteen, his cap pulled down to his ears, wearing high boots, spinning in a circle of curious idlers. Out of his boot he slides a booklet of obscene transparent cards which he sells for two sous and brandishes before their eyes with a conjurer's sleight of hand. 'If you see the arms of the City of Paris coming along on a *képi*, ladies and gentlemen, drop me a hint, so I can know where to go and wait for them.' For the police persecute them like the street-women whose lovers they are.

Pierre Hardy, having worked all day in his office, was strolling among the passers-by on the Boulevard Sébastopol. But a young man of twenty, only six months in Paris, walks with little assurance amidst the passing show of Paris. The winding vehicles, the blatant lights, the crowds in the streets, the lust and din create a frightening, Babel-like confusion and set too many ideas whirling simultaneously. Every provincial, indeed, has felt this uneasiness, and confronted with it each has become awkward and sad. I assure you that the handsome lads who strutted so jauntily on their village greens cut a sorry figure on the Grands Boulevards.

A man walks carrying with him all the properties of his

life, and they churn about in his head. Something he sees awakens them, something else excites them. For our flesh has retained all our memories, and we mingle them with our desires. We pass through the present with all our luggage, and wherever we go, at whatever instant, we are complete.

Here are the thoughts that accompanied Pierre Hardy on this July night:

Because he was twenty and had been living in Paris only since January, Pierre Hardy liked to return in thought to a house in a small town in the eastern provinces, where his parents were wood-merchants. This house, surrounded by a garden, was on a hilltop, a short distance outside the town. It was pleasant to be there on a summer evening when breezes cooled the shadows and one sat in the garden and breathed the night. Stars filled the mind, and at times the heat would make an effort and there would be flashes of lightning. Life was sweet and peaceful in the bosom of his family, as he smoked his first cigarettes. Every detail was charming. In the evening, if it were too hot, instead of eating soup, you had milk: a refreshment that refreshes you all the way to the heart. Sometimes the elder married sister and the little niece came for a week. One more course for dinner and a little more gaiety in the air. And the younger sister would play at being Juliette's mama. He took her out for a walk and bought her sweets. Nothing was lacking. Every member of the family was conscious that they formed an entity in happy nature.

He thought too of those three years at technical school. He had learned to draw bridges and machines with intricate lines and to brush on the washes, making each shade distinct and admirably blended. His parents had framed and hung up in their room a fine drawing showing a railway station between two hills. He had come out Number Two from the school, with a diploma and a silver-gilt medal.

He was able to procure a position at a hundred and fifty francs a month as draughtsman in a railway company. He regretted that he had not attended, as his professors had advised, for examination at the School of Arts and Trades. His parents would have made this sacrifice and he would soon have reached the grade of head clerk.

Along the Boulevard Sébastopol, with its file upon file of electric arc-lights, Pierre Hardy walked amongst the thousands of passers-by. The lights pierced through the foliage of the trees, and fell through the shadow of the branches upon the pavement. It seemed to him that the lights were brighter, and the crowd still more dense. Young men from the provinces feel lost among a hundred thousand people. He did not know a soul, and he kept on walking, and new people passed, all alike in their indifference, without so much as a glance for him. He was surrounded by their noise as by a multitude to which he did not belong. He saw them in masses, with eddies and gestures, gay like peals of laughter his ears had caught in passing, bright as those glances he had seen gleaming in women's eyes.

He sought to cling to something, so as not to be submerged. He felt the need of going deep into himself, there to discover some joy to set against all that passed before him, so that he would not be lost in the universal gaiety. He wanted to erect a dyke to withstand the mounting tide, and cry out: 'I too exist. I rise up in stone and cement, and I stop you while you howl.'

He lived in a small hotel in the rue de l'Arbre-Sec, in a room on the fifth floor. So many people have lodged in such rooms that they are habitually filthy. The bed, the wardrobe with its mirror, the table on rollers, the two chairs, fill up the room. The rooms are so small that the five pieces of furniture seem cumbrous. There you can live, for twenty-five francs a month, a life entirely bereft of dignity. The mattresses are grimy, the window-curtains grey as a day from a poor man's life. The hotel boy has a pass-key which enables him to enter your room at any hour of the day or night. The neighbours change once every fortnight, and you can hear the slightest sound through the partitions. Some are drunken, brawling couples, others have an odour of prostitution, and if some are well behaved, they still hardly inspire confidence. The poor lodgers in these small hotels have no home, no privacy, Pierre Hardy could not say: 'At least, I have a refuge where I can go when I feel sad and sit among the things I like.'

His sole refuge was Louis Buisson, with whom he had made friends his very first day in Paris. He was twenty-five years old and worked as a draughtsman in Pierre Hardy's office. A short man, barely five feet high, he had been exempted from military service because of his puny size. Because of this, he did not inspire his companions with much respect. They considered him a good sort, but his importance was in proportion to his height, barely five feet. He had been a former candidate for the Polytechnic School, and his study of mathematics had given him the habit of analysis. Until his twentieth year he had remained as a boarder in a provincial *lycée*, and this had given him the habit of suffering. Disappointed in his dreams of a brilliant future, he had grown modest. And he thought: 'I make a hundred and eighty francs a month. I live like a man of the people. I work to earn the bread I eat.'

His evenings were spent in studying literature and philosophy. First, he went out for a walk and looked at the young women in the streets. He said: 'They run after what glitters: rich young men and handsome young men. The rich young men give them a taste for luxury, and the handsome young men betray them and teach them that love is a foolish pleasure. Eventually, they return to us. With their clothes

and their theatres they ruin us, and they haven't enough
fervour left to become our sweethearts and companions. For
my part, I've taken up with a little servant girl. Because she
is simple and a hard worker, we'll set up house together.
I want to live like a man of the people, with a woman of
the people. Besides, I hate the rich because they rob us of
our pleasures.'

He had his own furniture and lived on the Quai du
Louvre, in a room on the fifth floor. Pierre Hardy confided
in him all his emotions and all his adventures, and Louis
Buisson did the same. Friendship such as this gives us
courage for life, prolongs our pleasures and consoles us in
our griefs. They said to themselves: 'I'll tell that to Pierre.
He'll have a good laugh.' 'I'll tell that to Louis, and he'll say:
"My dear fellow, we suffer because we're poor and shy,
and above all because we're honest men".' Between the two
there was a slight difference in education. Pierre Hardy
lived in the rue de l'Arbre-Sec, which is a Paris street. Louis
Buisson lived on the Quai du Louvre, where the air is
certainly freer.

But there are evenings when friendship does not suffice.
The words and the humdrum things of friendship rest us,
but we also have a need of tiring ourselves. Pierre Hardy
in the midst of the human torrent felt a little joy which came
to him from his friend. And looking at the crowd passing
by, he thought: 'You haven't a friend like Louis Buisson.'
But this did not console him, and the Boulevard roared
back: 'Far better to have a woman!' And again he thought:
'I am studying to pass the surveyor's examination for
Bridges and Causeways. No doubt I'll be promoted to
head clerk. Most of these young men passing with women
on their arms will remain petty clerks all their lives.' But
the passing crowd cried back at him: 'Who cares? We have
women, and we enjoy life.' He answered: 'I have a mother

and a father who love me more than these women love you.' 'Who cares?' said the crowd. 'You are alone and lonely. We have women and we enjoy life.'

Thus he was forced to admit that all the holiday joy was worth more than his solitary existence. He had nothing to oppose to the glitter of the lights, or to the overflowing of pleasure. Louis Buisson, in his zeal for two or three philosophical principles, derived from them strength enough to look men in the face. Moreover, he was seeking in them new laws and principles. But Pierre Hardy was twenty, and alone with a thousand desires, in the heart of a tempting Paris.

And often his desires swept him away. On certain nights, having studied until eleven, he closed his books and sat crushed with sadness before all their knowledge. All the diplomas in the world were not worth the joy of life. Two or three visions of women he had encountered came to his mind, and he followed them, at first merely to divert himself. Then all the fire of his twenty years flared to life, and his senses felt the magic contained in a passing woman. He leapt up, his throat parched, his heart contracted. He blew out the lamp and went out into the street.

He walked. Prostitutes pirouetted on the street-corners, with their threadbare skirts and their querying eyes. He did not even look at them. He walked as hope walks. A young woman with a pinched-in waist walked ahead of him, and, in order to see her better, he slowed down his steps. She turned and smiled. Then he lengthened his stride, the better to escape her, and because another woman with a pinched-in waist. . . He walked, as hope walks, from woman to woman. Some he did not want because they were too easy. Others he dared not accost because they did not seem easy enough. He walked, as hope walks, from woman to woman, until there was no longer any hope.

Sometimes a young working girl walked quickly past him, late and in a hurry to get home. She wore a black skirt and simple blouse, and there was no trimming on her hat. A young girl who, like a young man, worked and thought of love. Thus Pierre Hardy spoke naïvely to himself as he followed her, quickly followed her. He examined her, weighed her in his mind, pondering what measure of happiness she might give. When he had caught up with her he said to himself: 'I don't want to speak to her now because we're in too crowded a thoroughfare.' Step by step he followed her, turning all these thoughts in his head, following her with giant strides as one pursues an ideal. Far into the night, he would have followed her, for in her flesh she carried light. All these adventures came to the same end. Unexpectedly, the young girl stopped before a door and rang the bell. She had reached her home. He gave her one last look and went on, thinking of tomorrow, of all the tomorrows when he would never again encounter this happiness that he had just allowed to escape.

Finally, weary of having walked so long, he felt his old desires goading him. For the sake of peace, he took the first who came along, and on a sordid hotel bed, for the price of two francs, he poured himself into a dirty girl as into a public sink.

On this night of the fifteenth of July, the Boulevard Sébastopol was even more animated. People passed in couples, with slow, short steps, as though taking their love out for a stroll. Young men were saying: 'Her breasts were firm and small. I'll have to get hold of her again.' Paris, always on the move with its roaring traffic, the songs of its drunkards, and such a galaxy of prostitutes that there were tempting ones amongst them. The arc-lights were surrounded by haloes which, encroaching upon each other, illuminated the spaces between the houses and formed a

channel wide and luminous that overflowed the roofs,
mounted the sky, and there tossed up its fire. This atmosphere bathed you in a subtle fluid, in an electric and penetrating bath. Then warm winds, the exhalations of a summer
night, made Paris a howling beast, sweating and with
frenzied eyes, puffing until it almost fainted. One cry
answered another, someone in passing aroused a desire, the
lights set it blazing like a thing of straw. Each living being
swelled out upon the Boulevard, and cried aloud, like the
beast of love, to the depths of their dying hearts.

And Pierre Hardy remembered them, these hunts for
women. With shame he remembered them, under the lights,
among the thousands who passed and re-passed; and yet, at
the same time, he felt them deeply, as a man feels the great
principles that guide his life. Before his eyes walked Woman
with her sex, her sex open, as Louis Buisson said. And
suddenly Pierre Hardy was nothing, nothing. Paris, overflowing her banks, bore him on, swirled him into her eddies
and swept him off—Pierre Hardy, a wood-merchant's son,
Louis Buisson's friend, candidate for Surveyor of the Bridges
and Causeways—swept him away between her two lost
shores, swept him away to the end of the world.

At the corner of the rue Greneta, a crowd had gathered
round four street-singers. It was not yet ten, and at a last
street-corner they were singing perhaps their last song. The
father was scraping away at a red wooden fiddle, which
made considerable noise with its raw grimacing voice. His
eyes shot with sparks and blood as he surveyed the circle
of loungers. The mother, her belly swollen from her con-
finements, and her breasts bloated like a worn beast of
burden, had in her ravaged face two blue eyes, like two
dirty flowers. She sang in the shrill voice of a scolding shrew.
And the two little children, who had sung all night, could
hardly stand on their trembling legs. One glared about like

a vicious beast; he resembled his father, and in his fatigue he was ready to turn and bite. But the other, with his yellow face and blue eyes, would have preferred, like his mother, to fall prostrate where he was and go to sleep. Paris had ground them in her mill; she had ground them all four, the good and the bad.

Mothers and daughters listened. Three little factory girls bought copies of the song and followed the words. Some passers-by had idly stopped, and others glanced at the singers and went on their way. The crowd was small because there had been too many songs. Pierre Hardy stopped. You must look at something, so you look at this.

There were a few prostitutes as well, for crowds afford many an excellent opportunity. And the ungainly voice of the red violin rose above the three other voices, evenly, mechanically, insensitively.

The song cost two sous. Pierre Hardy bought it. He was reading it with great attention, when next to him a little woman who was also reading it said: 'That's not the real song.' He glanced at the young woman and saw that she wore a black band around her head and that she looked nice. This touched him, and he said: 'How does the real song go?'

'Like this,' she answered, and sang a line or two.

It was all the same to him, but a young woman with a ribbon in her hair can lend an interest to many things. So Pierre no longer listened to the singers. He said to her:

'I'm sure you sing very well, Mademoiselle.'

'Not now,' she answered, 'for I have a cold.'

It would soon be ten, and the wretched voice of the violin wailed on and on until the order should come for it to cease its wailing. They left the group of loiterers, and, as the young woman did not seem timid, Pierre offered her a glass of beer. He was very much afraid she would refuse.

It was like this that Pierre met Berthe on the night of the fifteenth of July. He smiled because she was nice and because she wore a black ribbon in her hair.

CHAPTER II

At half past twelve, when Berthe Méténier got back to her room in the rue Malebranche, Maurice, her lover, was already in bed. He conscientiously opened half an eye and recognized her. She undressed. The candle was burning on the night-table, and she went over to it to examine a little pimple that was annoying her above her knee. Then she dived into her left stocking where she kept her money, and, having taken out Pierre's five-franc piece, she laid it beside the candle. This time, Maurice opened both his eyes.

'Is that all you've made since eight o'clock?'

She replied:

'Well, why don't you have a try yourself? You'll see it's not so easy.'

Shrugging his shoulders, he turned his face to the wall. It's stupid, he thought, to have a woman who doesn't know how to work.

She came to bed, after blowing out the candle. Maurice was not too annoyed, for he himself had made something on the side. At the wine shop, he had met his friend Paul with a young man who was willing to play cards. Both he and Paul had managed to win one franc fifty. Besides it was only Wednesday. Berthe had three days left in which to make seven francs to pay the rent of her room. Thus they would have six francs fifty to spend next day.

He was not tired. He turned towards Berthe and put his arm around her neck. She kissed him full on the mouth. For a man and his woman this is a good and wholesome thing, and provides amusement for ten minutes or so before going to sleep. She made every effort to have her pleasure at the same time as his. Everything went off well. She never washed when it was with her man.

Afterwards she said:

'You think it's easy. There's more than one of them who won't bring back five francs tonight. I met a fellow who only wanted to give me three francs at first. Then he consented to give me five if I stayed an hour. I like that better. One gets regular clients and it's more respectable.'

Maurice did not answer. She went on:

'Oh yes, I know. You're always bringing up my sister Blanche because she comes home with fifteen francs. Well, after that she has her bit of fun with young boys and doesn't do a stroke of work for three days.'

Maurice did not answer.

'I could get hold of two-franc fellows, too. There are plenty of that sort after me. But I'd have to walk the streets all night to make a bit. And, as it is, you think I come home too late.'

She had a great need of approval. She was weak and needed someone to lean upon; she was gentle, and she needed kind words said to her. She would have liked to talk a long time. But he knew that in business one must always seem exacting. Women wouldn't do another stroke of work if you listened to their chatter. He answered:

'Shut your mouth. I want to sleep.'

Maurice Bélu was born and bred in the Plaisance quarter where his mother kept a small shop. Till his sixteenth year he remained in school, for it does no harm to acquire a little more knowledge, and it is always soon enough to send children into apprenticeship where they contract evil habits. He received a careful education, left school with an elementary diploma, and went about with boys his own age who gave him the nickname of Bubu. He was apprenticed to a cabinet-maker in the Faubourg Saint-Antoine. There they

C

called him Maurice. One day, on leaving the workshop, one of his old school-mates saw him and cried out: 'There goes Bubu!' This was not lost, for nothing is ever lost. Maurice again became Bubu.

He was a short man whose torso rested heavily on his sturdy legs. He would strike his chest saying: 'Small but husky.' His head was bony and his two eyes, stubborn, resolute, were slightly hidden by his cheekbones. His most prominent features were two arched jaws which, as they ground his food with a crackling noise of bone, nerve, and muscle, revealed their entire structure. This does not mean that he had an enormous appetite, but rather that he bit into food with decision.

In the days when his mother sent him to school for fear he would contract bad habits as an apprentice, Bubu had made a certain number of acquaintances. Some were apprentices who, every night, roamed and made merry through the streets. Others were of a kind that it is a pleasure to meet in the street: little girls of fourteen, girls of fifteen and girls of sixteen. They are the daughters of parents none too strict, who educate the young by giving them freedom. They desire so many things, and those who see them make bold to offer them even more. You, rue de Vanves, and you, slopes of the fortifications, have seen Bubu pass on fine moonless nights. He learned to know the street as it is to those who roam, the street with its tables of merchandise where the deft hand can show its skill, the street teeming with adventure. He learned something else, even more useful: he learned how to handle women.

What had to happen happened one day when Bubu, then eighteen years old, made the acquaintance of a robust wench of the rue de la Gaîté. As she worked at night, Bubu had to arrange his day so his work would not interfere with his love. With that quickness of decision characteristic of him,

Bubu announced at the workshop that he was giving up his job as a cabinet-maker to become a furniture-mover. He announced this with pride, because his shortness laid him open to many a gibe, and this demonstrated to everyone that Bubu was as strong as a furniture-mover.

He liked his new job, for the day's work was amply paid. There was a scarcity of labour in this line, moreover, and if a man kept his eyes open he could manage nicely besides. For one thing, he never bought any more shoes. His knowledge of women increased with the robust Hortense. His mother did not always approve, but Bubu, who had strong convictions, found powerful arguments which kept her in her place, and even showed her several times that he was a man of action who did not like to be contradicted. He grew stronger in his chosen way, left Hortense on the road, and then attained his majority. He was exempted from military service, because of his feet.

It was then that Maurice Bélu made his preparations. To tell the truth, his ideas for the future were not precise, but he knew it was necessary to have money and a woman. These two forces of present life guide us towards the future. He demanded, and received, a sum of five thousand francs which came to him by rights from his father. As for the woman, he himself would attend to that.

The day of the Fourteenth of July came. Blissful day when the wine shops are bedecked with flags, when fire-crackers go off in the street, and the socialist-revolutionary committees celebrate their victories. At night, there is dancing amidst coloured lanterns, the cornets open their copper mouths, and the café tables invade the street by special permission of the government. Because it is the anniversary of its deliverance, the people allows its daughters to dance freely in the streets.

Berthe Méténier, a little florist-girl of seventeen, was

watching the ball of the rue de Vanves in company with
Marthe, her big sister, and Blanche, her little sister. The
black bands on her forehead made her face look pale, but
there was a soft light glowing in her eyes. Maurice asked
her to dance once, then again, and then a third time. They
danced beautifully together: they were about the same
height. He was very well brought up, she was very gentle.
He asked her if she would like to take some refreshment,
but she refused because she was with her two sisters. He had
her point out her big sister, Marthe. Then, removing his
hat, he went up to her:

'Pardon me, Mademoiselle, but since you are performing
the duties of a mother, I am going to ask you a favour. Will
you allow me to offer a glass of lemonade to Mademoiselle
your sister, and will you give me the pleasure of taking
something with me yourself?'

Marthe knew there was no danger in accepting an invita-
tion from a correct young man. They sat down and talked.
He was a cabinet-maker and could make as much as seven
or eight francs a day. Marthe was a laundress and Blanche
was serving her apprenticeship in the same laundry. As she
explained, they had wanted Blanche to learn to launder the
family clothes. They had four brothers. Two of them were
probably running about over there. Their father was a
widower. He was a house-painter, and suffered at times
from painter's colic and was not always easy to live with.
They went into great detail. Blanche, the kid, was amused
and happy and laughed aloud as she drank her grenadine.

Maurice made an appointment with Berthe for two days
later. She came but, fearing her father, she could not stay
long. They strolled about, chatting, and in a dark street they
kissed twice. On their second meeting, Maurice made her
a present of a gilt ring with a pink diamond. Their third
meeting they walked about arm in arm, and she consented

to follow him into a café on the avenue du Maine. Maurice
was in no hurry, for he was through with light love-affairs.
As for Berthe, she was like many suburban girls who have
already had plenty of opportunity, but who have, however,
bided their time, knowing that tomorrow will offer a better
one. She did not come to the fourth appointment. Next day,
Maurice lay in wait for her, and asked for a frank explana-
tion. She replied that her father had prevented her from
going out. He said:

'Mademoiselle, you promised. Considering our relationship is what it is, you did not have the right to break your
promise. No human power could have kept me from going
to meet you after I had said I would . . .'

She bowed her head with that foolish air of poor children
who in their meekness do not know what to say because
they are in fear of inflicting pain. The little lark was already
snared.

Maurice seemed an eloquent and sincere cavalier of the
kind young girls long for, and his loyal declarations indi-
cated that there were in him depths of loyalty. Certain
things he said, other things he left unsaid, revealed in him
a spirit of mystery and adventure. This in itself was tempting. Berthe, sweet and docile when Maurice had taken her
in hand, now sweetly yielded. They fell into the habit of
seeing each other every day. He strolled under her windows,
whistling in a special way: Fouillofu! Fouillofu! This she
heard in the secret depths of her heart, like a voice she had
long hoped to hear. She ran downstairs and hastened to him.

Finally her father found out everything. He said:

'I know that bird. He's a fine cabinet-maker. Gallivanting
all day around the quarter. I'd like to know when he finds
time to work! He seems pretty poor stuff to me.'

He worried no more about it because, being the father
of seven children, he had had plenty of trouble and had

learned that life is stronger than any will we have. He knew that the girls of Paris are adrift on a sea of temptation, and that their fathers, their fathers The Poor, can offer them nothing to save them from it. He knew that we are dogs and labourers, that we have nothing but our own misery in a world where misery is a thing accursed. Misfortune follows upon misfortune, all we can do is to bow our heads and complain. He thought: 'After all, that's her own business. I've warned her, I can do nothing about it, if that's her fate.'

One night little Berthe left the paternal roof, to go and live with Maurice. Her sister, Marthe, was then pregnant. Blanche, the kid, had stolen five francs from her boss.

Maurice and Berthe lived in a hotel in the rue de l'Ouest, in a thirty-franc room on the third floor. It gave on the street, and, with its blue carpet and its two arm-chairs, it seemed to them like a luxury flat. Berthe continued to work at the florist's. Maurice broke into his five thousand francs. Every week she brought home twenty-five francs and Maurice added sufficient so that they need deny themselves nothing. Every evening they had their coffee in a bar. Then they went to the music-hall, or to the ball of the *Moulin de la Vierge*, or to the *Gaîté-Montparnasse*. Berthe's circle and ideas were widening. She came to know Maurice's friends and their women. Maurice's friends did little work because they had women who worked for them, and because they knew enough people not to have to work. She saw the pimps and swindlers in their daily life and understood that if they did not care for work, it was because it is far wiser to care for pleasure.

They watched the human herd pass before them, and laughed because they had their elbows on a café table while watching the others pass. It was a windfall for the women if they made twenty or twenty-five francs in a night. On the following day they would laugh all the louder, first because of the money, then at the thought of the poor fools who would give women twenty or twenty-five francs. It was a windfall for the men when they brought off their job. On one occasion, Grand Jules returned from his expedition with a large piece of black silk. All his friends' women had their share. Berthe's dress seemed to her more beautiful because it had not been obtained in the usual way. If she thought of it in the street, she would burst into laughter as at a huge joke.

Grand Jules had served eight months in the Santé prison for house-breaking. He knew the world and where it leads. He knew that at the end of the world was the Santé prison and he looked this thought squarely in the face. He acted firmly in accordance with his will. He knew how to break a lock and could kill a man simply. Women surrounded him with love like birds singing the praises of the sun and power. He was a man who brooked no subjection, for his life was more noble and more beautiful since it embraced the love of danger.

Berthe saw all these things on leaving her father's house, at a time when everything basked in the glow of her love for Maurice. The first lover of a young girl of seventeen is the one who shapes her destiny. When she took the bus to go to work, a little weary she would close her eyes and think of Maurice amidst his pleasures.

When he said to her: 'I don't want to work at cabinet-making, I don't want to move furniture any more,' she felt he was superior to any job. He spoke of his mother whose ideas were limited to two sous worth of pepper and four sous worth of coffee. He spoke of her thus because he was broad-minded. He said to Berthe: 'A hell of a time you had at your father's, wiping the filth off your baby brothers,' and she was grateful to him for having rescued her.

Before the first month was over, he was beating her, but not from nastiness. This is how it was: Maurice, who had not a compromising character, rigidly classified all human things. Like the Emperor Charlemagne, he placed on one side the ideas he did not like, and on the other those he liked. He thought: 'This is false, but this is the truth.' Like the Emperor Charlemagne, he had no feeling for shades of difference. It seemed incomprehensible to him, for instance, that anybody might wash his face before his hands. He said to Berthe: 'You touch your face with your dirty hands. That's a funny way to wash.'

One day she was frying eggs. She put in the salt and pepper immediately after breaking the eggs. Maurice knew that the eggs should be seasoned after they were cooked. 'Oh, leave me alone, won't you,' she said somewhat sharply. But Maurice, a man of action, believed in the necessity of corporal punishment. He slapped her, convinced a slap would assist her to see things in their true light.

Other times he beat her because she had displeased him, because he was angry, or because she was stubborn. Poor Berthe, with her gentle nature, accepted her punishment in tears. She was sorry then she had left her father. About this time she discovered that all Maurice's friends beat their women, and she understood that the ruling law of this world is might. She realized all that was contained in the words 'my man'. A 'man' is a government that beats us to show us who is the master, but who is able to defend us in times of danger.

Maurice believed that intelligence was related to energy, and that consequently his woman was not intelligent because she was gentle. He told this to no one. On the contrary, he liked to make her snap out at him before his friends, so as to prove to them she was hard to manage. And they thought: 'He's small but husky.' However, he loved

her a lot. He loved her because she was pretty. In the evening, when she came home from work, he could hear her
coming upstairs. He recognized her small hurried step, and
he could imagine her wriggling a bit so as to come more
quickly. He loved her smiling and gentle eyes that approved
all his desires. And her red lips, somewhat soft, that pressed
close to his. And her long black hair, and her head-bands,
and the chignon above her nape which gave her an air unlike
the others. And a voluptuousness, all her own, when she
strained her body to him, bending it so he could reach
deeper into her. He loved all that distinguished her from the
women he had known, because it was sweeter, more delicate,
and because she was his woman, his own, and because he had
had her virgin. He loved her because she was well bred,
because she was honest and looked so, and for all the reasons
for which the bourgeois love their wives. For Maurice had
bourgeois ideas. This is the price paid for attaining the age
of twenty-three without a police record.

Time went by. Two years went by and with them went
Maurice's five thousand francs. When five thousand francs
are spent after two years of life in common, our fate is not
shaped in one day, but its course has already been determined by every gesture we have made and every person
we have met. For a long time Berthe had already known
that those who are public prostitutes act no differently from
the others. Maurice would have liked to arrange things
otherwise. He resigned himself, however, and without much
suffering. He had a sense of property, but like that of a land-
owner who leases out his land. Berthe made no protest the
night Maurice brought himself to say to her:

'By the way, my little one, if anyone makes propositions
to you when you come out from work, better go along.
It will put a little more money in our pockets.'

And then at first the demon shows a smiling mask. In the

beginning Berthe made ten or twenty francs, merely for a 'moment', because Maurice did not want her to sleep out. Money was plentiful again. Berthe did not find the work too arduous, for she was always home about ten. Nor was it hard on him, for she did not keep him waiting very long.

Shortly afterwards she left the florist's, no longer wishing to work ten hours a day for four francs. She went out every evening about eight o'clock and did the Boulevard Sébastopol and the Grands Boulevards.

Thus it was that Berthe Méténier became a public whore and Maurice a man with no visible means of support. He was intelligent, he lived in Paris where pleasure howls aloud in passing. At first he had worked, then he understood that those who work and suffer are dupes. He became a pimp because he lived in a society of wealthy people, who are strong and who choose their professions. They want to buy women with their money. Therefore, to provide them, there must be pimps.

CHAPTER III

THE day after his meeting with Berthe, Pierre Hardy felt a little calmer. This little woman, whom he had had for five francs for a whole hour, had been yielding and pliant, as he imagined women one does not pay must be. Because he was poor, he had for some time now considered pleasure in terms of its cost. He knew that woman is greedy and that with a turn of her thighs she takes the entire earnings of a man's day. He was the son of thrifty parents, and if he sometimes lacked the will-power to forgo pleasure, he at any rate regretted the expense. But when he thought of Berthe's body and a certain electric pressure of her arms when they made love together, this memory was sweet as a little of that voluptuousness one expects at twenty. And since we live in a world where pleasures are bought, Pierre considered that this pleasure was well worth five francs. He made an appointment with her the following week. An appointment for half past eight in the evening, at the corner of the Pont-Neuf and the Quai du Louvre.

Pierre was the first to arrive at the rendez-vous. Presently he saw her coming. She wore a white straw hat, and the thick chignon of her black hair made the whiteness of her face stand out with unexpected sweetness. Pierre felt a kind of pride stirring in him. He would have liked to stroll about with her on his arm and run across a friend. He said to her:

'My dear little friend, I'm so glad you came.'

She smiled like the poor little whore she was; the smile granted those who pay.

'Really?'

The evening was mild and uncertain.

All along the Seine there was a gentle breeze that flowed

like water and seemed to follow the leaves. The shadows, lightly swaying above the passers-by, seemed to speak to their souls and gently cradle them. Everything was restful and because of that one loved it. The Seine, the sky, and the carriages shone with a modest radiance, and the line of the quays, with its rows of trees, seemed a country lane in which one could stroll and find solitude.

He said:

'Let's walk a little.'

She replied:

'If you like. I'm in no hurry.'

They chose the Quai de la Mégisserie.

Pierre was saying:

'I saw you coming with your little steps. You move your legs under your skirts, you wriggle a little, you smile and you look very sweet. It's easy to see you're good-natured. I would have recognized you among a crowd of women just because of that, and yet I've only seen you twice. But I feel as if I know you well.'

'That's very nice, what you just said to me,' she replied.

'It's the same with us. We prefer going with people we've already seen.'

They walked arm in arm, talking into each other's eyes, and Pierre was thinking they looked like two sweethearts. This little woman, so slim and pliant, was like the women seen in the street, passing with men who squeezed their waists. When evening fell and they were there, the world was full of desire. Lord, send us little women like Berthe so that we may kiss them, and that their twenty years may enrich our kisses! Pierre no longer remembered that this pleasure would cost him five francs.

A little beyond the Hôtel de Ville, the two arms of the Seine encircle the Ile-St-Louis, and form a broad river. This sheet of water flowed on, passed over the reflected lights, and continued on its way with the drowsy motion that water has. But the air, vaporous and green, rocked gently above it, as far as the melancholy point of the Quai Bourbon.

The world was calm and silky like the air and like the water. The boats, lit to the depths of their souls, split the water's gown with a wide, accurate gesture. Beautiful lovers pierced by the beauty of the world! Pierre also felt radiant to his very depths.

'How beautiful the Seine is!'

And he said again:

'Look at the sky. Over there I see two or three hundred tiny red clouds. It makes me want to pay you a compliment. In my heart there are two or three hundred little emotions burning because of you.'

She smiled and asked:

'What does it mean when the sky is red like tonight?'

He replied:

'Where I live they say it's a sign of war. But I don't think we two are going to have a quarrel.'

They walked slowly along the Quai de l'Hôtel de Ville, each conscious of being beside the other. The trams passed with their: *Ouan! ouan!* like savage beasts. But this noise meant nothing to Pierre, for Berthe caused a far greater sound to stir in him. The houses, lower down, seemed far away, and the passers-by on the other pavement did not intrude. He walked beside her, his heart brimming over. He said:

'This reminds me of my own town.'

This was not true, but he was near a woman and wished to make her understand his tastes and his life. He wanted to reveal his heart to her, so that she would think: 'Here is a young man with a noble heart who comes from a country of shadows and of love.' He wanted to draw her to him by his confidences.

'This reminds me of my own town. My parents' house is there, surrounded by a big garden. In Paris, you don't know what gardens are. In the evening it is good to be alive. You drink milk and eat the chickens out of your own farm-yard. There's a small river and a big forest. The trees in the forest are cool. I have a friend who says: "They are green like youth and so cool you'd think they made the wind." My little Berthe, I'd kiss you in the forest paths. We'd sit down on the moss and, without anyone disturbing us, we'd play at all your games.'

She said:

'I don't know the country any farther than Clamart. The doctor wanted me to spend three months there because of the good air. Doctors imagine one can afford all their remedies.'

And again he said:

'We're both walking along these silent quays. I don't feel at all uneasy when I'm with you because you let your-self be led and you let yourself go. You're not like a lot of them who go about it quickly and don't even want to talk. It's bestial, with them. They make it too evident that they're working and that work is not a thing to trifle with.'

And he repeated:

'I don't feel at all uneasy when I'm with you. You're not very talkative this evening, but I talk because I'm happy. You'll see that I'm a good fellow, and that I can do all sorts of nice things to please women. I kiss them like this, to make them laugh, and I could love them all my life so they'd be happy. But you, I liked at once. You're just as tall as my young sister. I used to take her for long walks and tell her my stories. I'd like to tell them to you too because you're sweet and I feel I can trust you. I'd like to tell you every-thing I know. I'm all alone in Paris, but I'm not really un-happy. I work and I write home and they write back to me.

It's always mama who writes. She can't write very well but when she says: "I love you dearly, dearly, my Pierre", I feel these words weigh like whole sentences.'

'As for me,' said Berthe, 'I lost my mother when I was sixteen. She died when I was in the hospital. They didn't want me to see her. Chlorotic-anaemia, that's what I had, and you can imagine that didn't cure me. I said to myself: now that my mother is dead, I am going to be unhappy. I didn't cry at all because I had too much pain, but I felt her death in all my limbs. She loved us dearly. Sometimes, on a Saturday, she'd say to us: "Come along, children, I'm treating you all to coffee!" And we'd go to the café with my sister Marthe and my sister Blanche. The children played near the door. I enjoyed myself because there were lots of people.'

Then she said:

'If you don't mind, let's go home now. I must leave you at ten o'clock. If we don't go now I won't be able to stay with you long enough.'

They turned back. Pierre let go her arm and put his own around her waist, and as he walked he pressed her to him. He drew close to her flesh as he had drawn close to her heart. He touched all of it that could be touched: the swing-ing hips, the pliant waist that bends and weighs on the arm, the soft breasts, already ripe, like the hearts of prostitutes at twenty. He touched everything he could touch, but he would have liked to touch more. He would have liked her to be quite naked, to feel her, to kiss her all over and taste her flesh. All the currents of his blood billowed into great red waves that swelled his senses like bursting ripe fruit. A short while before, he had thought to speak to her of Louis Buisson, of his mother and of his sisters, so as to pour the very depths of his soul into hers. Now she alone existed in the world. Facing her, he was about to kiss her lips, and already he felt his body bursting.

But Berthe scarcely talked. She did not talk, and could not talk, of her desires and her life. She listened to Pierre. A prostitute, gentle and still new to the trade, she was capable of generous thoughts: 'This young man is kind and he talks like a lover.' But it was impossible to take advantage of his kind heart and ask for more than five francs because that was all he had to spend. As for love, she had worn it threadbare. She knew what love meant since she had let the males chase after her, for they took advantage of every weakness and satisfied their most sordid lusts. She knew that love must be converted into cash, because love is wearing and money alone comforts and revives. Berthe knew all this at twenty. Those who have enough to live on seek out love because it is good, but prostitutes curtail their clients' love because it is harmful. And Pierre, this big passionate boy, was to Berthe only one more man to undergo.

She thought of her lover, Maurice, of her dress and of her shoes. Last night she had had to pay for her room. The owners of small hotels do not trust women who live on love. She had had to pay. But she had not been able to give seven francs, because five was all she had. She was granted a day's grace to get the remaining forty sous, but it was understood that if she did not pay she could not go back to her room. Consequently, at midday, they ate left-overs from the day before, but, this evening, she had eaten nothing. Maurice had said: 'You're an idiot. You'll never learn how to work.' She was not hungry because in big families children's stomachs become elastic and can contract without suffering. Still she would have willingly had something to eat, meat and strengthening things, to counteract the weakness caused by love-making and sleepless nights. And here was Pierre offering her speeches! She didn't complain, because some clients were very coarse. She might, of course, have told him the truth, but she feared he would have deducted the price of the dinner from the five francs. So she contented herself with thinking: 'I've had nothing to eat tonight. It's rather a nuisance.'

And then her dress. The skirt was shabby, and the blouse faded. There were wonderful things at the Carreau du Temple for twenty francs. Her sister Blanche had bought a silk dress, and moreover she wore it badly.

Her straw sailor hat was soiled and out of shape. But it was her shoes, in particular, that troubled her. In this business where you walk so much, heels get run down, soles wear out, and the leather splits . . . But she had to have pretty shoes! For an elegant shoe accentuates the shape of the leg when the skirt is lifted to attract a man. There was no doubt that within a couple of days Berthe's shoes would fall from her feet. Fortunately, the weather was fine. She started calculating to see if, after having eaten tomorrow and the next day, she would still have enough to buy a pair of shoes. She would have a look in a second-hand shop in the rue des Prêtres-Saint-Germain-l'Auxerrois, where bargains could be found for three francs.

Berthe pondered the details of her life as a prostitute. She reflected that after working tonight with Pierre, she would have to work with another man, and tomorrow she would have to make two more. The day after tomorrow she would have to work for her dress, and then for her hat, but by this time her shoes would be worn out. Days of fatigue are succeeded by days of exhaustion when day after day is spent in walking. Boulevard Sébastopol and the Grands Boulevards, with their long straight pavements, are hard as stone when you have paced them for many hours. Nowhere a little charity to be found. This young man would make use of her at least twice. The others would want their money's worth. Men abuse and destroy our bodies to let us

D

have bread. And these ideas swarmed in her head like a world of small black insects that buzz and sting and do harm to little children.

They reached Pierre's door. On the threshold, he took her in his arms and said: 'I love you so much, my little Berthe!'

Then he fumbled in her blouse.

CHAPTER IV

At noon, in the hotel room of the rue Chanoinesse, a grey and dirty light filtered through the grey curtains and dirty window-panes that gave on the court. The wall-paper with its yellow ground, the ill-kept floor, the four pieces of furniture and the trunk, formed the home of a public whore and cost five francs a week. The unpainted wooden table permeated with dampness, the two broken-down chairs, the other table with the wash basin did not seem like old things, but sad and mildewed objects corroded by vice; and there was the unmade bed where the two bodies had left their impress of brownish sweat upon the worn sheets—this typical hotel-room bed, where the bodies are dirty and the souls as well.

Berthe, in her chemise, had just got up. With her narrow shoulders, her grey skirt, and her unclean feet, she, too, seemed, in her pale yellowish slimness, to have no light. With her puffy eyes and scraggly hair, in the disorder of the room, she too was in disorder and her thoughts lay heaped confusedly in her head. These awakenings at midday are heavy and sticky like the life of the night before with its love-making, its alcohol, and its torpid sleep. One feels a sense of degradation in thinking of the awakenings of former days, when ideas were as clear as if they had been washed by sleep. Once you have slept, my brother, you too will have forgotten nothing. She still felt the weight of anguish which had, since yesterday, stifled her. She remembered everything, and it all pressed its two knees upon her chest, like a raging monster. And in truth, with her hollow temples, her wan cheeks, and her flaccid lips, you felt that she had few ideas and little courage, and you felt too that life was an evil thing because it dealt such heavy blows to children who do harm without realizing how far it may go.

She said:

'You know, Maurice, it must be what I thought. I spoke to my sister Blanche about it yesterday. She explained to me how it began, and it must be the same thing.'

He did not say a word.

She retraced her life, day by day, to the origin of the disease, in the need to know who had caused it. It takes forty days, she had been told. So she retraced her life from man to man, from basin to basin, living over each circumstance. The whole parade of love with its gestures and words filed through the hotel bedrooms. But she would have liked to plunge into the past, to halt it with both her hands and recognize this man, and blot out the day that she had known him. She thought she had found him, and then she told herself that it was all useless now, and that everything was useless. Then she gave up, and her sad thoughts closed over her.

Maurice broke the silence.

'I'd like to know who handed you that and break his neck.'

She dressed quickly, and then went downstairs and bought a bottle of wine and some sausage. They ate opposite each other on the damp table. The dirty carafe of lodgers who drink the slimy water of cheap hotels. Maurice, with bowed head, vigorously masticated great mouthfuls of food that swelled his jaws.

At the same time that he took his cap, he picked up the five-franc piece from the night-table and went out.

The August afternoon that stretched to the blue sky lay like a heavy cloak upon the shoulders. He followed the Quai aux Fleurs where the flowers thirsted, and where the flower-women sweated placidly while looking at the passers-by. The heat weighed on his head and burdened it with a shapeless weight of thoughts which he could not formulate, but which he felt all moving confusedly together. For the first time in his life, he knew indecision. Along the sparsely peopled quays, he, who usually walked straight to his goal without thought, now walked with no goal in mind, harkening to the sound of his own steps. He took the Quai de l'Horloge, walked the length of the Palais de Justice walls which stank of prison, crossed the Place Dauphine and the Pont-Neuf, and followed the line of the quays among the trees and bookstalls, walking with ponderous strides as if wishing to trample on his thoughts. He looked at nothing, not even at the excavators and the masons at the Gare d' Orléans, not even at the river-steamers and the tugs. He walked powerfully through the flood of thoughts that descended into his limbs like men of action do whose thoughts are transformed into acts. At the Pont de la Concorde, he faced about, and again followed the line of the quays, and then took the rue Bonaparte to lead him towards Plaisance.

The word, the awful word that had been with him in his great strides, burst forth, and it broke like thunder as he walked, and then rolled in time to his step like the beating of a black drum. The pox, Berthe had the pox! He felt it at his side like a companion, red and bloody, like an unbelievable and ferocious guest. As a man beset by flames throws himself headlong into the water, so he plunged into the rue Bonaparte and climbed towards Plaisance. The pox, Berthe had the pox! He knew his enemies and could look them in the face like a man who knows no fear. And he could fight, and he lived his life without remorse or shame, and he accepted chance as it comes on the Paris streets, with theft, and crime, and prison. But the pox, Berthe had the pox! He would have liked to take hold of her and shake her, his eyes in hers, shake her until death and until victory. He thought of tragedies, of *Roger la Honte*, of bestial howls and of defeats. He recalled its scientific name: syphilis. It was this implacable and peremptory science which knows our ills and gives them names that he feared; because it looks on us and sees us, because it throws us into hospitals, because it plunges into our lives its words and instruments as though we were nothing but flesh, sickness, and death.

But this word, the pox, was still more terrible. Certainly Maurice was not afraid of words. Words are only ghosts imagined by the sick in mind, and beyond and above them there is life to be lived regardless of any words. He was a 'pimp', an 'individual with no recognized profession', and often enough this made him laugh. And 'Berthe Méténier, the prostitute', too. What did words matter, so long as one lived as one wished? But the pox! He remembered a story of his childhood. He was fourteen when one of his neighbours died at the age of twenty-two. And the old wives said: 'He died like a dung-hill. They say he was completely rotten.' To be completely rotten . . . Other childhood memories and ideas of purity came to his mind. He had never been ill. His mother, who came from the provinces, would have said: 'Those are diseases we never had in our families.' To be completely rotten . . . He imagined red, oozing sores, lint and bandages, and he saw himself stretched out on a hospital bed, his body green and completely rotten. One day, when he was a cabinet-maker, one of his companions had said: 'If ever I get the pox, I'll put a couple of bullets through my head.'

In Plaisance, he went straight to his mother. She lived in her grocery-shop a prudent and busy life. She seldom sold more than two sous worth of stuff, for the big 'supply stores' swallowed up all the money of the quarter. She sat by her counter serving her customers and chatting in the familiar, garrulous way of small tradespeople.

A neighbour, who was there, said: 'I think I see your son.'

He had that exaggeratedly polite manner which makes people judge us with more tolerance and keeps our parents from disowning us. Then he went into the back room. He leaned his elbows on the table and all the objects in the room danced to the beat of the tune of his pox-ridden head. He usually looked on these objects as one looks on a petty life, thinking of his own free ideas and enjoying his sense of superiority. But this time, Maurice, a stranger to remorse, saw how peaceful it was in this back room and saw, too, what a good thing peace was. Meanwhile, the chaos in his head danced madly, and, like a bit of wreckage, endlessly whirled from chasm to chasm, whirled and danced.

He shook off this nightmare.

'Give me a glass of wine.'

She was afraid he had come to ask for money. She said: 'You look sad.'

He drank and replied:

'Yes, I feel like hell today.'

Then he got up and left.

He fled, and walked down the rue de Vanves. And as he walked among the black, populous houses, past the shops and bars of his youth, while the carriages clattered over the cobbles, he saw the people of the suburbs go by, from the working-men's wives who squawked in the street, to his comrades in blue smocks with their women, public whores, who laughed as they walked by their sides. Life was awakening and coming feverishly into being, with the cries and the haste of some, and the drink and the love of others. The air was pungent as it is at the doors of wine-shops and at the doors of wholesale groceries. Then, in this Plaisance quarter, he thought of his friend, Grand Jules, and he felt hope reborn in him. It is a mystery how hope is suddenly reborn. You are walking along the rue de Vanves on an August afternoon, and you remember that Grand Jules has had the pox, and you remember that Charlot, and Paul, and others have it still, and you think that the pox has never done them any harm. And then you think: 'But there's no proof that I myself have the pox.' And then you try to persuade yourself that you couldn't have it, because Berthe spoke out at her first symptom and since then you haven't touched her.

Thus he reached the avenue du Maine, familiar territory. There were bars where his friends would be. Maurice was on the point of looking for them when, on a café terrace, he espied Grand Jules.

'I was thinking of you. And here you are.'

Grand Jules was sitting alone on the café terrace, drinking a *café-marc* and watching the avenue. His cap was set squarely on his head, his head was straight and strong, and he watched the things and the people passing, with his ideas steady and calm like himself, each in its proper place, steady and calm, holding their heads high. Maurice sat down beside him. Although he was short, Grand Jules liked him because of the stubborn will that stiffened his jaws and muscles. Maurice ordered a glass of wine. Before them filed the passers-by, and, to fill in the time, Maurice and Grand Jules passed judgement on them with a curt and frequently ironic phrase. It was like the day of the Creation, when Adam, the king of the world, sat at the foot of an oak and watched the animals pass, and scrutinized them and gave them names. Finally, Maurice could hold it in no longer.

'The pox, you've had the pox. Does it put you on your back?'

'Got the pox?'

'No, but it's hanging over my head.'

'Ha, ha, ha!' laughed Grand Jules. 'That's not where it hangs! The pox wouldn't hurt anyone. I've had it two years. They made me take pills when I was at the Santé. I never had anything. By the way, you know her, it's Francine who passed it on to me. I didn't have to go back to her, I was told beforehand, but you don't ditch a woman because she has the pox.'

He went on to explain that it gave you spots on the skin and sores in the mouth, and that it went away of itself. Seated on his chair, he explained the pox in simple words, and when he had spoken, his thoughts went off on something else. Neither prison nor the pox had ever troubled him, for his will was stronger than any affliction. He picked his way adroitly through the midst of danger, and he fought without anger and without heat once he had made up his mind to the combat. I say that he was stronger than the pox.

He was astonished, moreover, that Maurice did not have it already. 'We all have it,' he repeated. Maurice ordered two *marcs* and emptied his own glass at a single draught. If he hadn't his dose yet, it was time he left Berthe. Possibly, he didn't have it, as long as she had spoken at her first symptom. Women go by, one after the other, and in such numbers that a clever man need never be in want. These tortuous ideas crawled through his brain and seemed to encircle it. But Grand Jules's ideas, brought forward with so sure a hand, took life before his eyes, and he saw them standing erect, side by side, and marching on. He emptied his glass of *marc* at a single draught.

Each paid his round and they got up. It was four o'clock. They went down the avenue du Maine, walking slowly, staring with the boldness of bullies, their hands clasped behind their backs. On either side of the broad avenue, the houses seemed low, the shop-windows seemed shabby, and the passers-by seemed few. For this reason, Jules and Maurice seemed taller. The measured step of the landlord, the confidant glance of the master, they were in their own quarter which they knew like a part of themselves and over which they possessed certain rights. Maurice recovered a little of

his faith: 'I am Maurice, who is also called Bubu of Montparnasse.' In this quarter where he had taken his first steps,
he felt as free and nimble as on the first day, and looking
at the things around him he thought how he had understood them in former days, and that today he understood
them better still because he had more experience.

Faith. He who looks into his own soul, imagining all sorts
of evil, recovers his pristine powers and feels they are eternal
and will combat all evil. They met Cécile, wearing an apron
and no hat, at ease, like them, in the quarter's streets.
She was dark, a bit heavy, with pronounced features, and
the sight of her brought knife-stabs to the mind. She said:

'I'm ditching Machin. He's talking of shaking me off.
I said to him: "Don't make me laugh! You've never set
the Seine on fire."'

Grand Jules smiled because she was one of his women.
He refused to keep any with him, but, in the round of his
operations, he had acquired certain claims upon their love.
He picked out one every night on his way home and took
her to bed with no waste of words.

Maurice smiled because he was far superior to those who
are ditched.

Then he recovered all his faith: 'I am Maurice, who is
also called Bubu of Montparnasse.' He drew himself up,
puffed out his chest, and stamped his heels, feeling himself,
from head to foot, Bubu of Montparnasse. Grand Jules,
beside him, went his way, silent and full of glory like an
army on the march. Maurice now knew that the pox is a
part of the life of man. He had known it a long time, but
there are some things we know although they are not deeply
engraved upon our hearts. Like all men, Maurice had come
to full knowledge only after having suffered much. To be
completely rotten . . . These words amused him now when
he thought of Jules and all those who were not completely

rotten. Syphilis, and the science that pries into us to find diseases, ah, syphilis, and the science balked by our wills, like doctors who can be held up and robbed at street corners. And his mother and the grocery-store, a wretched occupation which bent and broke you in two for the sake of a couple of sous. These things are termed accidents. The accidents of the pox are like prison which can be avoided, or from which one emerges stronger and implacable.

And in his new joy, he began to hanker for drink. Drink, it is joy itself, and if you are already full of joy, drink is fulfilment and intoxication. They sat down opposite the Gare Montparnasse. Two absinthes. Great jolting carts, cabs with dancing panes, omnibuses and trams with their rolling thunder and their barking horns, the whistles of locomotives, the sweating passers-by, the ponderous five-o'clock sun, the dust of an August evening, the departures and arrivals, this movement of thousands created an inferno of steam cranes, wagons, men, vehicles, animals and packing-cases, with all the civilization of factories and rail-way-stations, and time passing, howling.

People said: 'There are two pimps, taking their absinthe', and they believed that absinthe sank quietly into the brain of a pimp. Walking beside Grand Jules down the avenue du Maine, Maurice had recovered his virile faith, and he walked, relishing in his consciousness all good and all evil. The knowledge of evil is as good as good fruit on the dusty road, and helps us to walk between the pox and prison, like great travellers without hypocrisy and without fear. The absinthe stirred this knowledge, shook it, with fever and happiness, in the brain. 'I am Maurice, who is also called Bubu of Montparnasse.' Maurice is a man who takes women in his hands and fashions them. He took Berthe, the florist girl, chose her virgin and beautiful, and made her his pleasure, and then made her his trade. He looks about him, understands things at a single glance, and for bicycles and pavement displays, his fingers are as swift as the flash of an eye. He knows the intricate science of locks: a twist of the finger and a turn of the muscle, and men are delivered to us like children, and iron safes like toys. He knows the silent steps that are known as wolf steps, and he knows how to penetrate the shadow with his eyes like burning coals. He knows the blows that wound and the blows that kill, attack and defence, and the blades of a knife that can open the way when a man is in peril. He walks the city streets without a care, while some suffer, and while others labour; he can conquer all things around him; as he walks, he seems a man walking at ease in his own house.

He felt free and fulfilled in his ideas, in his organs, in the life he thought, and in the life he lived . . .

Grand Jules slapped him on the shoulder.

'Hey, Maurice, don't go to sleep!'

He answered:

'I'm having a good time thinking about my pox.'

Grand Jules burst into laughter.

'Thinking about your pox, are you!'

He ordered two more absinthes.

The second absinthe filled Maurice with murmurs, broke like a wave and flowed over his heart. He felt it humming in his head with a thousand awakened thoughts which revolved, laughed, and sang. The echoes of good replied to the echoes of evil like voices calling one another, and like steps going away. Berthe leaned over to love him, and laughed for having the pox. The world was like a man, innocent and pox-ridden, drinking absinthe on the terrace of a café. Grand sentiments such as Love, such as Faith, such as Knowledge, walked crying aloud in the streets near the railway stations. Joy was everywhere, and each movement seemed a dance; men seemed small beside this dreamer, and

Life laughed like a woman intimately known, who bows before our will.

All of a sudden, he remembered the song. The song of consolation. Oh, old song of the pox, making music of the afflicted, and rendering us as sweet and poetic as the suffering of the stricken!

'De l'hôpital, vieille pratique . . .'

Oh, song, you contain a world of love and resignation, and you contain even more than resignation! You crucify us on our calvaries, you show us our sores, you sing of remedies and you laugh at affliction; because of us, you dance, and you convince us of the glory of our suffering! Oh, Blessed be you! Old song of the pox, in the hospital where you were born, you sang from bed to bed in every heart, you defied the dying, and over the brows of the pox-ridden, you brushed your wings, old song of the pox!

'To whom it hath been given to suffer, he it is who deserveth greater suffering.' It is these beautiful words you bring us. Are you the science of good, or are you the science of evil? You lay your old body against ours, you talk of mercury, and you talk of love. You say: 'Brother, behold thy sister who sits upon thy bed and lays her two hands upon thy healing heart.'

When Maurice left Jules, he took the rue de Rennes, and thought of going home. The cooler air of early evening stirred between the buildings and, refreshing the forehead, soothed the mind after the day's work. The sluggish passers-by felt their shoulders unburdened of their tasks and turned towards their homes and towards their women with the lucid emotions of summertime. Maurice felt a better man than usual. An alcoholic blood coursed in his limbs, now filled with animation, now suffused with kindliness. Why is the heart of man so large? 'I do feel funny tonight,' he said to himself.

He passed a large grocery-store and, looking at the wares outside, he saw some boxes of mandarins. Little mandarins, juicy little bits of nothing, you were never made for the coarse mouth of a bully. He passed another grocery-store, and this time he looked to see if there were boxes of mandarins. It's not such a difficult thing to do. First, the glance must not waver. No one is looking. Then, the gesture must be rapid and easy. Without stopping in his walk, Maurice slid the box of mandarins under his blouse. To give Berthe some pleasure, have his hands open to give her a souvenir, something of his own doing, a little of his love, a few mandarins for a small sweet mouth.

Then followed the thought of the pox. What if he didn't have the pox! What if he didn't have the pox! Then it seemed to him that this would detract in some way from his glory. He walked with so much passion that his legs seemed lifted off the ground. If he didn't have the pox then it was high time he had it. He walked towards his goal, the mandarins under his arm, his soul expanding and his voice so strong that it never occurred to him to cast a backward glance.

When he entered his room, Berthe was doing some cooking for the meal.

He said:

'Look here, I've brought you a box of mandarins.'

She smiled her astonishment.

'Oh, Maurice, something must have happened for you to be so nice!'

'Come and kiss me.'

She came close, and as she kissed him simply on the lips, he passed his two arms around her shoulders and held her there. In his turn, he kissed her mouth. Then he continued; once very hard, once gently, then very hard, then less gently . . . Meanwhile, he drew her to him, pressed her to his belly.

She said:

'Let me go. You'll have me burning my stew.'

He laughed.

'I don't care.'

He took her up with all his force, lifted her slightly, bent her backwards, and crushed her to his flesh. He was not usually in such a hurry. He dragged her, all dressed, to the bed. Berthe looked into his eyes in her sad way.

'But you mustn't, Maurice. You know that . . .'

He answered:

'What the hell do I care!'

When he reached her, he felt his heart melt, and he made himself very gentle, and he said:

'Does it hurt you, my little one?'

CHAPTER V

LOUIS Buisson lived on the Quai du Louvre, in a small square room on the fifth floor. There was an iron bed with four copper balls, a book-case in some light wood, a combination wash-stand and chest of drawers, a table covered with a red cloth, one chair, and two 'Armenian arm-chairs' which had cost twelve francs at the Bazar de l'Hôtel de Ville. A linoleum carpet covered the floor, two posters and a few engravings adorned the walls. This was the orderly existence of a young man who cleans his room himself and furnished it simply, in the image of his own soul. The window opened on a wide arm of the river, next to the Pont-Neuf and the little square where air, light and water afforded a variable and refreshing spectacle. Are we really in Paris? We are high in the air, in a country of water, but the air of it rumbles like the rolling vehicles.

On this night, Louis Buisson was making his coffee. He was thinking: 'Fixing one's room or preparing one's coffee are simple tasks which calm the mind and arrange one's thoughts like pieces of furniture in their proper place . . . ' He had, moreover, his own ideas about making coffee. He never used the old grounds but poured boiling water, drop by drop, over freshly ground coffee. This operation takes some time, but, if you want things to be good, you must take pains.

When Pierre Hardy knocked at the door, Louis Buisson did not wait to pour the coffee. Then he said:

'I'm quite put out. I've spoken to you about a little servant girl I had taken up with, and I hoped she would satisfy all my desires. Women of the people are simple, and all women can be moulded. I lent her a few books to shape her to my taste. She liked to read. I said to myself: "She'll learn to understand all those little refinements which make for order and happiness in a household. At night, I'll work at home. She'll rest herself doing some sewing, and I will feel her beside me like a small burning flame." Here's what happened. Yesterday, and the day before, we went out together, as her mistress was away on a journey. My little maid likes all sorts of good times, and she suffers at not being able to go to music-halls, and dances, and see the lights in the street. So I had to take her all over the place and after that she wanted to go to the Bal Bullier. Then I understood, I, who wanted to be a man of the people, that the people are over fond of evil pleasure. Perhaps I don't belong to the same people that others do, and that's why no one could ever understand me and enjoy living my life. I broke off with her. I thought that I had found the right woman, and here I am, all alone.'

Louis Buisson was somewhat dogmatic and talked at great length. They said to him at the office: 'Oh, you, you always want to be right! You make long speeches.'

They drank their coffee while smoking cheap cigars, and each of them, seated in an 'Armenian arm-chair', appeared to be an awkward and timid young bureaucrat. They were not happy, neither of them, because love disturbs young men of twenty, and because Paris is hard on the poor.

Pierre Hardy said:

'I was beginning to get used to my little friend Berthe and those five francs. And now she's sick in the hospital.'

Louis Buisson said:

'I used to know some prostitutes when I was living in a hotel. They have outbursts of gaiety like children who cry out so as not to be afraid.'

Pierre Hardy had much to learn from his friend. Louis Buisson was the interpreter of their life in common. He

E

analysed events with force and, at times, if he came upon an old error or a new truth, he was all at sea when he tried to adjust his conduct to his ideas. Analysis is not a bloodless science, but passes through our hearts and troubles them. Louis's emotions aroused emotions in Pierre because they lived their life in common and because their souls were open and sincere. Pierre said to himself: 'Funny, how he's always right.' He thought as his friend did, but he did not think so loud.

Pierre Hardy added:

'I like her much more since she's been ill. She writes me awkward letters but you can see she's suffering and that she's not so strong. She writes: "I kiss you with all the little heart of a sick child." I've sent her a little money. It seems to me that when she's cured, we'll be closer to each other.'

Then Louis Buisson set off on one of his long stories. He smiled as he thought: 'I am going to make a speech.' Then he said:

'We ought to love these girls who suffer. I always believed that if we can't save them, it's because we don't love them as we should. I used to know one who was just a novice. She was fourteen, and lived with her mother who had remarried, and whose second husband kept a wine-shop. There she made the acquaintance of a great strong lad with violent eyes. A mere look from him dominated her like a mighty power. One day she followed him to a hotel, where she meekly become his woman. She told me that afterwards he took her, stark naked, in his arms, and laid her in the middle of the eiderdown. She was so small that the eiderdown almost submerged her. She did not move, and she was so exhausted, that she fell asleep there with her virginity lost. I do not know why her parents had no search made for her. They lived together four months without her doing any work, but gradually he turned her from the path of virtue. He took her himself to the Grands Boulevards and picked out a client for her. She made fifteen francs and this gave her a sort of naïve delight.

'When I knew her she wasn't yet sixteen. I never saw a woman so brave about her work. She had finally managed to get work and sewed spangles. My dear fellow, she sewed all day, and she sewed all night. She wasn't sixteen. But she couldn't even make fifty sous a day. And the Other was there, behind her, with his two fists, and his jaws. Sometimes, when the rent was due, she had to go down into the street. I knew her. There were mornings when she came and asked me for two sous.

'The passing of time only brought her other miseries. Finally her mother got worried, found her, and had her closed up for a year in the convent of the Dames-Saint-Michel, where they put girls who have bad instincts. When she came out, her lover asked to marry her and her mother gave her consent. It's madness that rules the world. Then the past began all over again. And he deceived her, he took a special pleasure in deceiving her. One day, in Carnival, they were walking together in the crowd, when one of those women went by. He followed her and didn't come home for three days.

'Later they separated, but he came to see her from time to time and wanted money. She had a friend then, a young man of nineteen. "Even if I live to be an old woman," she said to me, "I'll never forget that boy. Not because he was rich, but for all he used to do for me." He loved her with all the kindness of his adolescent heart. One night when she was tired he carried her in his arms from the Place de la Bastille to the other end of the avenue Daumesnil. He liked going to her room when she was out and putting some pretty surprise on her table so he could hear her cry of delight when she came in. My dear fellow, this boy, who had servants to wait on him at home, and whose mother had her own maid, would go and see his little friend and, when she wasn't there, he would sweep her room and polish her shoes. Their love came to a sad end because her husband beat up the young man and he had to stay six weeks in bed.

'I've not known these things a long time, but each day I understand them better. There was once a young man so rich in love that he entered into the heart of one of these poor girls. And I, also, should have entered her heart. When the young man came, it was much too late, but I would have been in time. That's three years ago. She was not married and I could have taken her from the arms of her ponce. I should have taken her and brought her home and fought for her. I should have saved her. D'you understand? I could have saved her! Ah, why didn't I love her enough? I should have swept her room and shined her shoes. I should have been willing to stay in bed three weeks. There exists in the world a woman I could have saved!'

When Louis Buisson had finished his story, he put his head in his hands, and there was a silence during which each perceived there was no more coffee in his cup. The vehicles could be heard rolling by, five storeys below. Louis Buisson resumed the conversation:

'You were telling me about your friend Berthe, but you didn't say in which hospital . . .'

Pierre replied:

'She's in the Broca Hospital.'

Louis Buisson gave a start.

'But, my dear fellow, you don't know the Broca Hospital? I've seen all that and I can tell you that the Broca Hospital is full of whores. They are very sick. They have syphilis.'

Then Pierre Hardy felt Louis Buisson's story burning like

a fire in his heart. He saw things in their true light; a thousand things struck him at the same moment, mounted and drowned his voice like an overflow of evil. Then he had a feeling of rejoicing in peace because he had taken a step in love, a sorry jig one night, which now moved to the tune of syphilis and the Broca Hospital. He had that feeling of rejoicing in peace, seeing again the walls of his little house in the provinces and syphilis standing on the door-step. And he understood that until now life had seemed to him too easy.

Louis Buisson continued his discourse:

'I used to go to the Broca Hospital when one of my friends from the *lycée* was a dresser there. I saw all those women, with their diseases, prised open with the speculum. I saw little creatures from the Quarter with chancres, who laughed because they had been told: 'The pox is nothing. All you have to do is to take pills for three years.' I saw women who had had eighteen months of the pox and who were crying. They covered their heads with their arms and wept, saying: "I will never be cured." And the doctors consoled them with bursts of laughter. And I saw old ones, opening their legs like animals. Poor prey that they are, wounded, and submitting without complaint, long since accustomed to wounds.'

Thus Louis Buisson spoke, without a thought of Pierre. Then it came to him in a flash: But Berthe! Pierre and Berthe! . . . He looked at his friend who, with his two hands clasped on his knees was not thinking of making fine speeches. That poor girl with the pox, he saw her in tears, weeping the tears of the syphilitic, and it was so sad a sight that he could not make her a single reproach. The characters of young men of twenty are formed as much by their friends' words as by the impulses of their own hearts. Pierre reflected on all the thoughts of love Louis had expressed and, adding his own native generosity, he felt pity for Berthe and at the same time feared for himself. He was very frightened. He knew little of the pox to dare look it in the face, and only knew that people speak of it as of Shame and Evil.

Then Louis Buisson rose, went over to Pierre and, taking both his hands, he pressed them in his own. Usually he was discreet in his tenderness. 'But I have done wrong, Lord, with my talk.' He revolted against himself, against his own words, against truth, against the Broca Hospital. This cannot be, because it causes pain and my heart is good. He rose, went to Pierre and said:

'But no, Pierre. But no, no . . .'

He cried out, and he wanted to cry aloud, over the roofs: 'But no. No. No . . .'

When he got home, Pierre wrote to Berthe:

My dear, dear friend,

I am very unhappy as I write you this letter because you will be very unhappy when you read it. You are ill, my little Berthe, and I would like to be by your side to console you and to let you see that I am suffering because you are suffering. But there are some things I must tell you.

Before tonight I knew nothing about the Broca Hospital. I know now why you are there. You must be very sad, but don't go and think I will desert you. I never desert those I am fond of and I am fond of you because we have known each other for three months now. I am sending you a postal order for three francs.

Here is what I wanted to say to you: our relationship must change because I do not wish to catch your disease. I never hesitate to sacrifice myself, but this sacrifice would do me harm without doing you any good. But we shall go on seeing each other, won't we? We shall take walks together when you wish and we shall be two friends, friend Pierre and friend Berthe.

You must surely understand that I can't run after your sickness. I think I have escaped it, because I see no signs, but I am not yet out of danger. One of my friends, a doctor, told me this. I must wait a fortnight.

Berthe, if I were ill, I would forgive you. I come from a family where no one has ever had diseases like this. I would not like to pass it on to others. But we will write to each other as in the past. I hope so much that I will never regret having known you.

I leave you, my dear little friend, and I think of you. I await your reply with great impatience because I want to know if you are not too unhappy because of what I have written to you. I love you always and I love you more than ever because you are sick.

Your friend who kisses you,

PIERRE.

Two days later he received the following letter:

Pierre,

I got your letter which made me sick but I expected it the nerve to put it all on me but you think you can get away with it but you're wrong there I always knew you gave me that dreadful disease. But you're right I never said nothing because you helped me but now you think I have enough like this but I suffer I'm so sad I could die and you're happy at what you've done and to how many other young girls to who you give a few francs for their trouble of giving themselves to you you make them rotten. Perhaps these young girls have killed themselves like me if I hadn't thought about my family but I thought my father had suffered enough with my mother dying without hearing about my death also. Then I didn't think I'd meet my executioner one day boulevard Sébastopol July 15. The tears I've cried since that day but it's too late and I must resign myself and I say this because I'm sure you gave it to me and made the misery of my whole life. And I'm going to have more days of terrible suffering and others also will suffer and I pity them those people who have to suffer because of you for me the people who know you gave me this disease hate you more than me but I listen to no one's advice that's why I suffer in silence. You must know I'm not a dirty girl because if I wanted I also could make lots of men rotten but I prefer to take care of myself and when I'm cured I'll see what to do but never I'll forgive you. You don't deserve it a man who did me so much bad which I didn't deserve either and I didn't think one day I'd go on the rack for you know right now I'm suffering something awful in the throat at this moment. I know very well you don't care but this relieves me and you must know more than me what one feels with the head in this state and then the lint I picked up one day on the floor you don't wash your feet with it and then the ointment which is on the night table below the basin you give yourself frictions with it it's good for the pox and not for nothing else also . . . But the sickness exacts it or you'll have worse accident than you have and the woman who goes with you will get it at once but what is a nuisance is when you're excited an accident comes and you give it to others then you ditch her and it's another's turn and you are jealous because others have not got it bad like you. But Pierre I beg you take care of yourself like me and that way you won't give nothing otherwise you might get worse and injure yourself this is bit of advice. As for your doctor friend that is invention because you are through with me and that's all.

I hope you won't be too angry with me but you see I am
not wicked I only want one thing just to never meet you
for you are not a friend like you are you say less than nothing
or the pavement I walk every day but you will keep my
souvenir in your memory like I keep yours but like a man
not worthy to have a girl like me for I am the best girl one
can find in Paris and it's always like that. At last I dain to
answer your letter and tell you I think of you in spite the
hate I have for you:

Mademoiselle BERTHE

the girl and poor miserable creature who has only hate for
the man that made her rotten.

A fortnight later, the doctor found that Pierre had
syphilis.

PART II

CHAPTER VI

BERTHE remained a month and a half in the hospital.

Maurice waited for her as for his daily bread, and on Sundays and Thursdays he went to see her. She said: 'The doctors want to keep me here another month'—'I've hung around long enough,' said Maurice—'What can I do about it? I've got to get cured.' And he answered: 'Oh, I know! You always want your own way.'

He waited for her in the hotel room, sitting there drinking water from the carafe. Often, he ate Brie cheese. For three francs, he sold his umbrella, and for two days he waited with a certain assurance. A friend came along with a five-franc piece which paid for the room. Sometimes he ate at his mother's, but she refused to give him money. He said: 'You'd let me croak!' She replied: 'Go to work!' Berthe gave him a few fifty-centime bits: there are no expenses at the hospital. There were two or three women who offered him lunch, and bought him tobacco, but not one of them could become his life because he had made his choice, as men do—once and for ever. He had a woman or two, because a man needs that. Sitting on his chair, he waited, gnawing his fists, and eating dry bread.

He waited, whole afternoons spent in walking aimlessly through the streets. At times, the weather was gloomy and remained motionless above his head like a veil of ennui, like a dead and indifferent thing. The days of action with his comrades seemed gone for ever, the days of adventure and the good old times when he had lived amongst men. He had two or three memories: Berthe yawning, and dragging herself about the room, growing more and more sluggish. She said: 'I'm fed up.' And he answered: 'If you're fed up, I'll shove my fist through your face.' He had not understood how anyone could sit at home, inert, for an entire evening, while outside the world was restless and full of activity.

He understood much better now. A little pain throws light upon the evils that before we could not see, like better and eternal brothers. He felt, too, how precarious is happiness and that the heart is a black tottering ruin. He lost his faith, and wrote to Berthe: 'I'm lonely for you. This is the first time we've been separated and it seems to me we're separated for ever.' Poems did not come to him because he knew no poems, but one by one, all the love songs he had heard came back to him. The loveliest and purest were the best. More than ever before, he was moved by Beauty. Above all, it was the song of Lakmé that came and rested on the throbbing wound. It sprang from his lips like a cry, like an exhalation, like a good perfume:

> Qui, je veux retrouver ton sourire
> Et dans tes yeux je veux revoir le ciel.

But the day came when Maurice was even more weary of waiting. Berthe had been in the hospital for two weeks, and already his poverty seemed to have lasted a long time. In the first days of poverty there are friends and resources, but before long, when your shoes wear out and your clothes are frayed, the poverty of bread and water becomes the poverty of rags and tatters, the demands of which friends cannot meet. In the old days there was the belief in the possibility of adventure. It is all very well to steal when it is for pleasure, but he who steals through need puts too much fever into his adventures to carry them off with a steady hand. And then you get sick of dry bread. His belly was full of the memories of this, a preposterous weight of Brie cheese, the oppressiveness of hunger and bad food. Revolt growls in the body, the smell of cheese nauseates, and the strong man looks about him with penetrating eyes.

Then he saw his friends again. Not as in the old days when he spent his afternoons, gaily, his mind at ease in their midst. They went to back rooms and sat there, their elbows on the table, their fists under their chins, talking in low voices and drinking red wine. In him there was a gentle melancholy which kept him from accomplishing his daily acts; he had to have a great fire of battle, a great adventure, to stir and conquer him; in one day he had to recover all the strength of Bubu, and at one stroke accomplish all his daily tasks. There must be a great robbery that would put enough gold in his pocket for him to wait, like a profiteer of love, like a poet of sorrow thinking only of his lady and the fine morning of her return for new espousals.

It was a simple and disappointing tale. It took place in a tobacconist's shop, at three o'clock in the morning, in the heart of the deserted avenues, at the moment when silence encourages men and seems as comforting as a last word of advice. There they went, dry of throat, and with blood in their fists. Are you at last, the three of you, my brothers, about to stop your hearts beating, and see what can be seen in a robbery while the hand shakes, and seeks, and finds? All went well till they got to the cash-box: the door and the drawers had not been hard. They never had luck, not one of the three: Maurice had always suspected it. The box contained sixteen francs, the box contained only sixteen francs! Then they seized everything: stamps, stamped paper, cigars, cigarettes and tobacco. They filled their pockets, then their shirts, then they made packages with their handkerchiefs. When they left the shop, the avenue was still deserted, and the three of them separated, with the heavens over their heads and their thoughts heavy.

At the end of two days they had not sold many stamps
and they could not dispose of the tobacco. The sale of stolen
goods is as uncertain as the theft itself, and the days of nerves
on edge are terrible for a man *tête-à-tête* with his treasure.
Maurice walked the streets, his pockets full of stamps, and
packages of cigarettes on his chest. There might be friends.
The morning of the third day, as he walked along the Quai
de l'Horloge, two men came out of a corner. He had already
seen them the day before and noticed their heavy shoulders
and their mugs. He glanced back, and the two men were
following behind. He heard their shoes like heavy boots,
felt them heavy as fists, with the solidity of the policeman
who knows all. He tried to walk faster and more lightly.
Then the blood rushed to his head. This was foreseen. Two
formidable fists seized him, two shoulders shoved him, and,
in a nameless brutality, two voices to which there could be
no reply said:

'Come on, get going!'

He had his pockets full of stamps, and packages of cigarettes
on his chest.

Berthe heard it from her sister Blanche, one Thursday
night, in the visitors' room of the Broca Hospital. Blanche
had it from Charlot, who had it from Grand Jules, and, in
spite of prison walls, they also knew Maurice had just had
a syphilitic chancre. Blanche spoke in an excited voice, the
bearer of a great piece of news, with grimaces and gesticula-
tions and a kind of glory, like a newspaper announcing some
important information. There followed a full, deep silence,
in the black air of the hospital, between the four walls of the
visitors' room, while the sick suffered near by, and Berthe
felt alone in her solitude. An air of gloom oppressed every
head and veiled every eye. More than ever was the hospital

the hospital, and more than ever life was life for which you
fought and which wounded you sorely. Berthe understood
that life until now had seemed to her too easy.

But Blanche said:

'Well, what of it? He's been beating you up long enough.'

Berthe found that Maurice's habits had entered into her
body and, mingling with her blood, now formed her flesh
and mind. She was first of all Berthe, but she was also the
woman whom a man had watered for four years, as the land
of Egypt is watered by the overflowing Nile. She was very
frightened. When she was seventeen, he had taken her by
the hand and shown her the world. Then he had said to her:
'This is the way you must go', and he had watched her to
see that she did not forsake the path. The days in the hospital
were still Maurice's days, because of the Thursdays and
Sundays when he came to the visitors' room. And then she
knew that she might see him at any instant. But now,
everything spun around her: Paris, the hospital, the present,
the future, and a host of confused sensations:

'Un seul être vous manque et tout est dépeuplé.'

During the days that followed, Berthe sought to re-
arrange her life. She rearranged it with her sister, Blanche,
with a little friend called Adèle, and then with someone—
anyone—because a woman should not be alone. She ran-
sacked her memory for men. She remembered Pierre, whom
she had accused in her distress and who had written to her,
swearing he was not guilty. He had sworn as she liked oaths
sworn, on his mother's head—and this proved that it was
true. She thought of other men, too, and rattled them in her
head for the sake of the sound they made, so that she would
have something to hope for. But nothing could efface the
memory of Maurice and, had a god lain across her doorstep,

F

and had he made her his mate and exalted her to glory, and even had he made her rich, and even had she loved him, never—never—could she have forgotten him who was her own, and who was more than a god because he was The Man who had taken her a virgin. His flesh was engraved upon hers more deeply than all emotion and all desire. She did not know how men were judged in prison, but all the afflictions of the past had given her a great mistrust of the future and had taught her that disasters are begotten of one another. She was sick because she was unlucky, and for this same reason she believed that Maurice would be far from her for years.

Thus she felt she was lost, and all along the tomorrows she led her thought in search of some small piece of happiness that she might seize upon with open hands; she paused at every corner where it was possible to pause, but nothing satisfied her heart, because she came from a fair land that was her own.

CHAPTER VII

So one night Berthe came out of the Broca Hospital. A summer night, an autumn night? . . . The fine days were over. It was a night when Berthe had not a sou in her pocket. She sought out Pierre, as though seeking out five francs. He was studying in his room with all the tenacity of a man from Lorraine bent on success, but without enthusiasm, for the studiousness of solitary young men bears little fruit. He had answered her letter, forgetting her insults, and she had answered that she believed his word.

She came unexpectedly. But something stood between them, and each felt that, all around them, this thing was there. But you must master yourself, and waive scruples of honour when you are poor. And there was also that other thing which estranges men and women: she was thinking that she did not have one sou, and he was thinking that this visit would cost him five francs.

First, you must live, and afterwards you may indulge your sentiments. It was only the next morning, after she had left Pierre, that Berthe went for news to Maurice's mother whom she knew slightly.

She reached the little shop in Plaisance about ten o'clock. The other woman said:

'Ah, so it's you, is it.'

She went with her into the back room, and before sitting down she was already at it:

'It's for you, my son did that! I know all about it. You gave him your filthy, rotten diseases, and I know where you come from. Sluts like you, you're a curse!'

She went on a long time in this strain, hurling full, emphatic sentences at Berthe. In the back room, the waxed

furniture seemed to reflect her words and give them force,
like a moral example set up before the world's excesses.
Clean, and neatly combed, she spoke with the indignation
of a respectable woman, and at the end, since her son would
not forget Berthe, she hoped Berthe would not forget her
son, and would, from time to time, send him a five-franc
piece. Meanwhile, Berthe, with bowed head, stared at her
hands and blushed. Her head was filled with confused ideas,
and she listened to the old woman, not knowing what to do,
bowing her poor gentle soul and feeling guilty. Some days
she was so meek that she had no realization of the harm that
was being done her.

She went to her sister Blanche.

No one in the world would have taken Blanche for
Berthe's sister. She was a girl of seventeen, pink and blonde,
but if her skin were plump and young, her clothing and her
demeanour far removed any idea of youth, and she was
recognized by the pimps in the street as the prototype of
what is called a *môme dessalée*.

Her hair was cut short on her forehead and curled at the
temples into corkscrew ringlets, as was the custom with the
prostitutes of the faubourgs, in observance of the eternal law
which gives a uniform and upholds the pride of people of
the same trade.

She walked bare-headed, her hands in the pockets of her
apron, sticking her stomach out and dragging her feet as one
drags an old shoe. After the days of her childhood, when she
stole five francs from her boss, came the day, when in a
cheap hotel, she let her virginity slide into the hands of a
pimp; and in the days to follow, when all the instincts of
her flesh and mind drove her towards the same career, she
came to choose it of her own free will. She plied her trade
with assurance, acquired at once the right tone and air, and
was, in her first youth, the prostitute, as Monsieur de Musset

was, in his first youth, the poet. Syphilitic by vocation, no backward glance ever gave her cause for regret; she had a head full of lice and no desire for cleanliness, and her skirts enveloped her with an odour of vice and grime which brought men running from all directions. She lived, care-free and gay, and since money in this world is an end in itself, she had no idea of virtue nor honesty and, once her pockets were full of money, she felt as happy as a man who reaches his goal.

From among the ponces of the rue de la Gaîté, she chose one her heart fancied—an independent heart as variable as life itself—drew him to her, and when she was tired of him, tossed him aside and chose another, according to the evolutions of her desire. She was her own mistress, her own government, and she protected herself by the aid of a big knife which she always carried in her pocket, and which she fingered with assurance like a fearless traveller his weapons, knowing that his courage will never fail.

Berthe related to her the scene that had just taken place. Blanche said:

'What! You didn't talk back to her? I'd have given her a piece of my mind! I'd have said: "You old hypocrite, you're only too glad I feed him! You pull all that stuff because you know I'm a fool. He hasn't a rag on his arse that he's earned himself." Let him show his face here! You'll see if I know how to handle these bloody pimps!'

It was with her sister that Berthe lived when she came out of the hospital. With her sister, because family sentiment is stronger than any other, and because a sister is always a sister whatever happens . . . So it was here that Berthe took up her abode, with Blanche who was strong and who lent her a little strength. Blanche, like an example, went her way without occupying herself with others, and Berthe, bewildered, had only to follow where she led. She was sad at first because of her old habits, and in her simple mind, she thought: 'I'm lonely for Maurice.' She thought this very strongly as she looked at the things about her with some concern, as one looks at an old friend who has changed his clothes. She lived with Blanche, who relieved her conscience and said: 'It's you who's right.' However, it was not a question of being right or wrong, but we seek everywhere that reassurance for ourselves which forms so great a part of happiness.

At night, between nine and ten, they went down to the Boulevard Sébastopol. From the Place du Châtelet, it extended before them with its pavements and its two lines of lights, and it seemed to them an implement of labour they knew how to handle, and which they manipulated without fatigue because their bodies were inured to its play. Every street-corner spoke to them of memories, at each step their purpose walked by their side, and they belonged to it without a smile, without emotion, like tradesmen practising their trade. Blanche had the easier technique and called out to the men who passed. Berthe, writhing a little, only used her eyes.

The crowd: young men like question-marks, men of forty of grave demeanour, whose phrases were distinct and ringing like a five-franc coin; drunkards who could no longer count, who slobbered with love, and who fell asleep, and whom one left in bed . . . Pimps with their black jowls passed by, brushed against Berthe and Blanche with words, with mannerisms, as though flapping crow-like wings. They looked at them with the dry stare they gave a man who was not theirs, shrugged their shoulders as though the men had alighted there and they wanted to shake them off. They went on: Blanche bare headed, with the long, sturdy stride of laundry-women carrying their baskets, Berthe with small, mincing step, and the airs of a little florist-girl. Prostitutes

passed by: those who, young and dazzling like pleasure at
seventeen, do not know enough to take advantage of first
opportunities and rich fancies—those who did not stop in
the Boulevard Sébastopol but who went their way with
the rustle of starched underwear, sowing envy in their wake
—those who had had several years of the street, who knew
it well and who expressed its very substance—and, then, the
old ones with a heavy cowlike gait who stationed themselves at the street-corners and courageously stopped every
passer-by because their daily bread was at stake. The lights
served to study the faces in the street. The café terraces were
hunting-grounds where the girls scattered glances and
then turned back to see if they had reaped what they
had sown.

A little later, Blanche left her sister and went off towards
the Halles and the rue Montmartre. She liked to work alone,
for serious business required solitude in which to concen-
trate one's powers, like a man determined to succeed in life.
If anyone even glanced at her, she attached herself to his
heels, and, akin to that desire which lurks at the bottom of
our hearts, she came, she was already there, with her gestures
to satisfy our needs. She sold cheap so as to sell more often.
It was a district of newspaper offices and bars, and because
it was dark, men were easier. From time to time she revived
her spirits by drinking, for fifteen centimes, a cup of coffee
with a swallow of alcohol, and about four in the morning
she got back to Montrouge, her purse replenished, her heart
content.

On the Boulevard Sébastopol and the Grands Boulevards,
Berthe made a certain sentimental appeal. With the black
bands on her forehead and her white face, and her legs
swinging in her skirts, you felt her walk was like a graceful
action in a refined life, and her heart as tender as a young
woman's made for gentleness and love. Many a bird was

snared. Young men thought: 'She'd be nice at any time, for apart from that, she looks as if she knew how to talk and could appreciate what one said to her.' And they said: 'Mademoiselle, I am following you, and you're making me walk very fast!' And at times she thought up an answer: 'Oh, I'll tell you how it is, Monsieur! I'm very small, and when I walk fast, it's much less evident.' Other times someone would walk by her side, saying nothing, because she was this way, and his heart was touched. Then she smiled and drew him to her as sweetness draws. She appealed through sentiment to young men, and also to those more mature, because there is such a wealth of love here on earth, and because Love flows and carries us like children towards women who seem childish and kind.

She had syphilis. At this time, her mouth was very sore, and I think each of her kisses carried syphilis. Many a bird was snared. At the hospital, she had said to herself: 'I don't know what to do because I don't want to give my disease to others.' She came out. The first days, she thought: 'I'll say to him: "Wash yourself well."' But then she had to eat, and pity is not a thing for daily use. After walking a long time, the stones of the cobbles grew hard, and weighed on her steps like a burden of cobbles, and like hearts of stone. She thought: 'They gave it to me all right . . .'

This is nothing, Lord. It is only a woman on a pavement who passes by, making her living because it is very difficult to do otherwise. A man stops and speaks to her because You have given us woman for our pleasure. And this woman is Berthe, and You know the rest. It is nothing. It is a hungry tiger. The hunger of the tiger is like the hunger of the lamb. You have provided us with nourishment. I think this tiger is good because he loves his female and his cubs, and because he loves to live. But why must there be blood in the hunger of the tiger, whereas the hunger of the lamb is so mild?

There were young men, very young, who knew nothing and who went to women with all their heart and with all their money. There were young men of twenty-five who needed women, who sought them, and laughed when they found them. There were married men who thought: 'A little adventure, a smile, a moment's caprice with the girl passing by, because she is there, and because she is unlike what we had expected.' There were men of forty who took precautions. There were men who passed, anyone at all, any man who found himself there at a certain moment of his fate.

From Brittany a man of fifty came to spend a week in Paris on business. He met Berthe the night of his arrival. Every night, he took her to dinner, to the music-hall, and even to a cabaret now and again. Thus he came to know the night-life of Paris, which he had not known as a young man because he had had no money then. And he went back to Brittany, to his wife and his daughters, with a glowing heart and moist lips.

Another time it was a man of thirty-five who accosted her, and who had taken some time to accost her. They spent the night in a cheap hotel in the rue Saint-Sauveur and he gave her fifteen francs. He said to her: 'Before coming to bed, fix your bands nicely around your head.' He lay down beside her and kissed her eyes. 'This way you are like a woman I loved very much, and whom I lost.' He did nothing else, but leaned on his elbow, and she went to sleep. And all night long he passed his fingers over her bands. Thus many a beautiful heart is saved.

Usually Berthe went home at two o'clock, because then the streets had nothing to offer but the chance of forty sous, for at that hour feelings were weary.

Often Blanche picked up near the Halles 'her man' of the moment, who did not always have a place to sleep, or who was watching the night's events. The three of them, he, Blanche, and Berthe, slept side by side, but Blanche kept in the middle so that her man would not have diverting contacts, and because she was jealous. It was a hot and sticky night, with Blanche's sighs, the man's assaults, and Berthe's shaken and jostled slumber. Then, in the morning, the unclean male and the two stuffy women stretched, shook themselves, and, towards noon, got out of bed. If Blanche went down to fetch some food, the man, alone with Berthe, made the most of the minute's freedom and started the attack because Berthe was pretty, and because an opportunity must never be lost. She protested, then let him have his way, was frightened, and laughed.

So Berthe was a prostitute. This is not a business you leave in the morning and, once far removed from it, become yourself again like a clerk when he has left his office. Do you know the odour of vice once it has entered the lungs? The fists of the pimps mould these girls and leave their marks upon the white flesh beside the desires placed there by God.

They live, and form a great herd, side by side, Blanche, Berthe, and all the others, and each serves her neighbour as an example and a lesson. There is the air of prostitution which at first smells of liberty, and which then sinks and stinks like a thousand sexes all day. And the evil enters under your skirts with its devouring kisses. There are the pavement, the hotel rooms, and the silver coins, an entire trade wherein you sell your soul at the same time as you sell your flesh.

There is the happiness they seek out. The happiness of the prostitute is like those faces in the street which are strong and which bite into life with their tough jaws. They want a happiness wherein men stand erect and overcome you with

their fists like a burst of anger to which you yield. There is
the love that they seek out. The love of the passers-by comes
and goes, leaving no trace of its passage, but for a woman's
heart, there is the other love, the love that seizes them and
bends them back and makes them fall. In the old days,
there had been Maurice.

Thus it was that Berthe sought happiness in love. First
she knew Blondin-le-Cycliste. Blondin-le-Cycliste was big,
broad, and red; his hands were firm and his feet were strong,
and he walked the street with a massiveness which his eyes
seemed to press upon a woman's breast. He went in for some
sort of traffic in bicycles, and on one or two occasions auto-
mobiles passed through his hands, and this gave him the
skilful air of a mechanic, and the industrious air of a trades-
man who is superior to the common run of trade. He took
Berthe to the country, and this, too, made him different
from other men. At times, his pockets were full of money,
at other times, as Berthe put it: 'he needed a little help.' His
rough and urgent love at times brought her feasting and
abundance, and at other times it subsisted on the forty sous
of the woman he loved. And you loved him because he
made your bones crack in his arms, and you gave him
everything because he didn't want to be taken for a fool.

She knew the Aztec of the Grand-Montrouge, one night
when she was going home. He stood at a street-corner, pale
and slim, his jaw thrust out and his will taut. When he
accosted her, she knew there was nothing to say, and that
a man can do anything he wishes when he looks the world
straight in the eye.

She knew La Quille, one afternoon in a bar. He limped,
and seemed to be a pimp at loose ends. Five and three make
eight, lame men are funny, and this love was a sort of a lark.

And she knew many others: the lads of Montrouge, of
Montparnasse, and those of the Latin Quarter; loves of an

idle afternoon, loves on her way home at night; she knew love even on the Boulevard Sébastopol, love made in haste between two clients. She went rioting and boozing through the bars, drank anything that was offered to her, paid everybody's drinks, roared with laughter as one does because binges are a sort of uproarious holiday. She was a bitch with dogs sniffing her thighs, jostling one another with their things erect, and the palpitating tongues of dogs in heat. She knew them all, walking the streets, weak yielding flesh that she was, without buoyancy, without a nerve to tauten, without a belonging of her own. She tossed her purse into the air, and the pieces of silver poured out of it and were sucked into the torrent of vice that knows no curb.

She knew Kiki. Kiki was sixteen with a shrill voice, and in and out of your legs he twinkled, as kids do. He was a bit of a costermonger, and he knew the street as it is known to those who make their living on it, giving false measure, and holding his own with the customers he cheated. Men did not take him seriously, and because of this Kiki reacted with his teeth and claws, snarled in the streets, seized upon things, and felt, more than others, the need of showing-off. Once he met a nurse with a child. The child had a whip.

'Give me your whip so I can make it crack.'

Kiki amused himself with it for five minutes. Then the nurse wanted to go and take the whip with her.

'Nothing doing,' said Kiki.

As she stepped forward to take it from him, Kiki drew back and cracked the whip in the girl's face, saying:

'Keep away.'

The child cried. Kiki went off cracking the whip, turning from time to time to jeer at them. When they were out of sight, the whip was in his way, and he tossed it behind a fence.

He was a tough little kid for tough little girls, one of those mosquitoes whose stories made you laugh. And jokingly, Berthe let him have his way, and this was wrong, for a woman who has any self-respect chooses a man who is good for something.

Now and again, Berthe met Grand Jules, and at first he always stopped her and talked to her as to the wife of a friend. He called her 'Madame'. But when he learned of her conduct, he no longer spoke to her and, his head erect, he watched her pass, as a soldier on duty watches those who violate law and order.

CHAPTER VIII

THERE were other days for Berthe, the days she went to see Pierre Hardy. He said:

'You have done me a lot of harm. I met you one day; we were both twenty, and I suffered because I was a man. Twenty, it means love; but love, it means money. I took a little love out of my savings. And right away I got that disease. My poor child, it's neither your fault nor mine. We live in a world where the poor must suffer. I was neither rich enough nor handsome enough to choose my woman among those I knew. You know very well I took you by chance. As for you, I think you must have had a lot of trouble, because you hold out your arms to everyone who passes by. It consoles me a little to think that one day it was I who was your daily bread. I'm not a very intelligent man, and in the beginning I hated you. But a friend told me things that I repeat to you. I learned that the world is evil and that we were both to be pitied. You have done me a lot of harm. Today, it is the harm you have done me that should bring us together. You are the only woman possible for me, because my touch gives the plague.'

Berthe replied:

'What d'you expect? That's our trade.'

They had dinner together in a one-franc-twenty-five restaurant. The tables were covered with a white cloth, seated six, and seemed to be, with their glasses, their carafes, their cruets, well laid-out tables where you could eat the fine dishes of the rich: minced venison, chip-potatoes, mirrored eggs, floating islands with chocolate cream. You saw men with high silk hats, moving with formality and pride, eating without a word, holding themselves aloof,

profoundly aware that they were clerks at the Hôtel de
Ville. There you could eat all those sauces invented by
vanity to ruin the stomachs of the poor. And you ordered
your food in a tone of command and conversed in a low
voice because well-bred people make no noise. Berthe was
impressed by this luxury, and she, who had known the cheap
delicatessens of the faubourgs, said: 'It's not too bad here.'

But after dinner, in some near-by café, they would take
a cup of coffee. The time was far better: they chose a corner
and, their elbows on the table, far from people who made
a noise and people who showed-off, they had long conversa-
tions. Berthe, the rolling stone, who rolled her way through
vice, sat in a corner, her elbows on the table, and from the
depths of her consciousness rose a small, sad and tranquil
flame. Pierre looked at her and, feeling a woman at his side,
thought he perceived a little love, a small straight flame
which burned and seemed so frail. From the first they spoke
with utter frankness. She had need of this because in the
soul is a good corner which, in the days before doing harm,
is replete with simple emotions, and there it remains forever, and at times voices descend into it, and come crying
like forsaken children. She had need of this as we need a
mother, and then a husband, we who are women with no
support, with uncertain hearts, who seek certainty on the
high roads. She felt the need of saying: 'This is how I am.
Look at me and tell me what you think of me.' There was
never any love between them, but there was something
which surpasses love: there was trust and kindliness.

She talked about Maurice and told him everything. She
had a lover who was called Maurice, who was vicious and
slapped her constantly.

'I don't know if I love him. He's beaten me so much that
I never asked myself.'

He was crazy. One night when he was beating her, he

felt he was going to kill her. He had time to seize a pillow, throw it on her head, and he struck it with his fist till he was worn out. Next day her face was all black and blue. But now he was in prison.

Pierre could see him. He saw these things at twenty and bowed his head, as Adam, when he saw there was evil in the world. Lord, there is much evil in the world. There are women beneath Your eyes who are Your children. You have created them, and You put them at our side for our hunger like a pretty cake. They seemed so delicate that we dared not lay our hands upon them. Lord, Lord! And there beneath Your eyes women who bear iron crosses. Lord, look upon Berthe: there is a man astride her shoulders. He holds her in his claws and buries them in her flesh lest she escape. He forces her to walk. With all his weight, he bends her to the ground, so she be weary as a broken beast, so that she neither behold You nor hear Your voice.

Pierre looked at Berthe. He said nothing. He took her hand and held it in his fingers, so that his pity might pass from him to her, very simply—like this—so as to comfort her a little. Then they went away. He took her to his room, and in the street he kept her hand, so that no one should come and touch her. He leaned towards her, and added a word or two so she would understand how it was:

'My dear little friend, my dear little friend!'

Sometimes Louis Buisson joined them at the café. He sat on the other side of Berthe, and the three of them, their elbows on the table, drank their coffee, like three young friends come together for a talk. One of them was a poor child, one of those who does not know how to comfort you, but who brings you a little clarity, because you feel he wants to so much. The other had more understanding of your illness, and when he put his finger on it, you felt a finger both electric and gentle, which touched you out of kindness and probed you because sores must be probed before they can be healed.

It was about this time that Louis said to Pierre:

'I am reading the Gospels. One night, Jesus went up to the Garden of Olives with His disciples. It was a night like these Paris nights when we know that pleasure is evil because men put into it no love. He looked over Jerusalem where harlots and debauchery clashed like evil weapons which slay you so that you may forget. He remembered that the world is full of money, and that princes, priests and soldiers hurl into it hatred and blows. He mounted to the Garden of Olives to say to His apostles: "I am Love, Let us meditate up there and keep watch, on the eve of my death. We shall pray Him who guided me to your path that He keep me with you a little longer. And tomorrow, when I shall be dead upon the tree, you will set forth into the world and you will say 'Love is born and we have come to bear the glad tidings'." Then He went and prayed for a long while. Then He wanted to speak again with them. And he turned and saw that they were asleep. Peter and John and Judas and Thomas and all the others, their arms over their heads, they were all asleep as though they had nothing to do but slumber. Then Jesus felt that the night of the earth had covered him. "For years I have been spreading my soul over the world to bring it life. Forgive me, my Father, but I see that all has failed. Those yonder sleep today, the last day You have granted me. If the best succumb, if the good are too frail for the Good Word, why then did You send me? There is not enough human warmth. I have preached burning love and my poor love is about to die."

'And I thought of Berthe, Pierre, because of what Jesus said in the Garden of Olives. Christ, on His last day, may

G

have wept, but the Good Word is still alive. The sleepers
had preserved it, for the Spirit is strong if the Flesh is weak.
They have saved several souls: Saint Francis of Assisi, and
Saint Vincent of Paul. And we, my friend, we have been
found by a prostitute. We will teach her that her life is not
good, and we will put a little more kindness into our own,
so that she may understand it and love it. I do not know if
we can save her, but I know that there are no limits to the
Good Word. If we fail, my brother, let us console ourselves
with the thought that we will have cast a little light into her
soul, and for all we know, we may have been the beginning
of her salvation.'

And then later, when he sat beside Berthe, he asked her:

'Tell me, my child, why do you still keep on with this
sort of work?'

She gave a foolish smile, like children who know the
answer, but who are afraid to speak. Her eyes fell, but for
some time the smile played on her face. She said nothing.
Anywhere else she would have said: 'Oh, come off it, don't
make such a fuss.' She would have said this because those
who show interest in poverty begin by taking advantage
of it, and then forget about relieving it.

But Pierre looked at her as though to say: 'Come, my
little friend, you know I'm here with all I possess.' And all
he possessed radiated around his face like a hearth aglow
with beautiful lights where you felt the heat that was about
to come. Then she said:

'You think you can suit yourself in life.'

They asked her questions. How much money used she to
make in the flower business? She answered that you could
make a living, because you were paid twenty-five francs a
week. You can get a little room for five francs and at night
you can cook at home. A woman, it's not the same as a man.
She can manage all right by herself.

'But tell us, my child, why do you keep on doing this sort of work?'

Here's what she'd do: When Maurice had a little money, she would set herself up as a florist. She'd have two working girls and she would pay them twenty or twenty-five sous a day, and they would bring in three times as much. Then she launched forth into all her stories: she had met a gentleman who was going to take her to Russia; she knew a young man who was giving her dancing lessons, and then afterwards she would get a job in the Moulin-Rouge dancing in the quadrilles. She was going to sing in a music-hall where she would wear a low-neck dress, like this, with a blue silk blouse. Maurice wanted to buy a gramophone, and the two of them would do all the fairs in the neighbourhood of Paris. She would have liked to have been a sales-girl in a tobacco-shop. 'Demi-londrès? Here you are, Monsieur,' she would have said, smiling.

She launched forth into all the stories of the poor little run-about whore that she was. Her imagination took great strides and it was pleasant to ramble on like this, successful in every enterprise. Men say to one another: 'You turn the crank and then watch them talk.' When you know the world, it's a rest from your worries to listen to children prattle.

But Louis Buisson said:

'My child, when you are unhappy you must come and see us. You will tell us your stories and I know it will give you pleasure.'

Then, wishing to work, he left them.

And Pierre said:

'You must come. Days when you're sad, you must come to me. You'll say: "Oh, I'm so lonely, so lonely!" And I'll look into your eyes and answer you: "As for me, there are days when my heart is breaking with loneliness." You must know how happy it makes a man and a woman to suffer together. I'm all alone, and when a friend comes to see me, it seems to me that I'll never be all alone again. In the evening, you can find me before dinner, and have dinner with me. After that, you can find me at the café. You will become my little heart. It's you I missed. Don't be afraid. Women are always thinking one wants to take advantage of them.'

Thus he spoke and deep in himself he thought: 'It's so good to have a woman by your side.'

Many times she came. The first days, she was afraid, and knocked meekly at the door, like an ant scratching with its claw.

'I've come to see you. I had an errand close by. So I said to myself: "Suppose I go and see Pierre?"'

At first she came before dinner, because hunger will drive a wild animal from his lair.

She made apologies at the restaurant:

'I beg your pardon. I'm helping myself to salt before you.' There is much timidity in our hearts, and even if one is a prostitute with a wanton heart, one is none the less a woman among men, a woman with all her gentleness and hesitation.

A little later, she said:

'I came to see you, and I know you won't be annoyed.'

Many times she came. She came when she was sad, with a bit of debauchery and the brutality of bullies clinging to her skirts. She came on days when she was ill, turning her miseries over and over in her mind, like a never-ending litany of despair. She came on days when she was weary, her limbs drained, her back aching. She never came when she was gay, because then there were the streets to run wild in, the pimps whose joy was more substantial, and the money

of prostitution to scatter over all the bars. Mostly she came
on rent day, with her trade and her need of earning her
bread.

'How are you?'

'Look!'

She showed him the tongue, and the palate full of disease,
which all night long and every night gave kisses to the
passers-by and slipped spittle into their mouths as though it
were a delight. Her throat was sore and her voice rasped as
it passed by something that festered there. She had pains in
every bone of her body, and they seemed to issue from her
very depths as though from a reservoir of pain. Moreover,
she refused to take the mercury pills, because she had heard
that mercury brought the disease to the surface.

She came some nights, not having eaten since the day
before. This was not apparent, for the face of misery is much
like any other. First she drew herself up in a sort of pride
and ate no more than usual at the restaurant: 'After all I
mustn't make him spend money.' But after dinner, her
mind and her body sated, she could contain herself no
longer. 'You can be sure that it's not what I ate at noon that
could give me a stomach-ache.'

Pierre said:

'You hurt me, my little friend. You know so well I am
in the world, and near you. So come, please come. Truly,
it is good for a man to help unfortunate women. This is
called: relieving suffering humanity. When you haven't
enough to eat, think of me. You need say nothing. You will
come, and I will understand.'

She answered softly:

'It doesn't matter. I got up this afternoon at three and so
I didn't feel at all hungry.'

One night, it was in December. A savage December that stamped through the streets with ice and wind, like a tyrant trampling our manhood, that cut to the marrow and there remained, more powerful than any happiness or grief. A Paris December, when the prostitutes huddled their shoulders close to their bodies, shrank in their clothes, and blew in the wind with the flames of the gas-lamps. Pierre was working in his room. The stove purred like a good old faithful cat and seemed to say: 'It's all right, master, I'm here.'

Pierre thought:

'It is a shameful illness and it radiates like evil.'

And he thought too:

'New Year's day is coming. New Year's days are very different now. I shall ask my chief for a week's holiday and go home to my village. Mama will say: "Here's our Parisian!" And the old women will say: "We don't dare say *tu* to him now." My two sisters and my little niece will be there. Every night, I'll be in the good warmth of the provinces which penetrates into our hearts and hatches our thoughts like little chickens. This is my first year of syphilis. I will kiss everyone and drink in glasses. And they'll say to Juliette: "Along with you, greedy girl, have a drink out of your uncle's glass!" I will kiss them near the hair where the lips press more lightly. But afterwards I won't know what to say about my glass. Mama would say: "He'd have to go to Paris to catch those putrid diseases!" And my father would say: "He's fine company for his sisters!" and all those who couldn't get jobs in Paris will be glad.'

And he thought:

'I must pass my examinations for surveyor of Bridges and Causeways. Otherwise they'll think I no longer care to work. And I work and eat mercury, not knowing whether, when the time for tertiary symptoms arrives, I may be allowed to live.'

In the midst of all this, someone knocked at the door. Pierre got up and already forgot his troubles because it was Berthe, and because a woman is always what a man needs. It was Berthe. As she came in, she brought winter in her cold skirts. She said:

'It's me. It's nice and warm here.'

Then: 'Oh, listen! D'you know what's happened? They've taken my sister Blanche to Saint-Lazare.'

It was on one of those bicycle merry-go-rounds. Blanche, with her mania for always doing just what she liked, was kicking up a row as she rode around, showing her calves and all the rest. 'We'd told her often enough: " Better not do that or they'll put you into quod some day." Well it happened just as I said. At the Police Station, they had the medical examination. She was not healthy, so they sent her to Saint-Lazare to be taken care of.' And Berthe added:

'Of course it's me now who'll have to pay the room.'

She sat down and said nothing more. She came very close to the stove, so near you might have thought her insensible, or mad, and, her two hands clasped on her knees, there she remained, with her head bowed. Under the hands on her brow, she appeared a poor little woman made of flour, a poor little worn-out shape, leaning forwards, all forlorn. And she gasped:

'No, no, no! It's been going on much too long!'

It was very sad to see her so. All the causes could not be fathomed, because causes overflow and hang above our heads their hundred thousand iron fists whose weight mingles and is weighed together with the days, with the sorrow, the blows received, with the harm one has done, and with the vagabondage of the nights. And a night comes when all is over, when so many jaws have closed upon us that we no longer have the strength to stand, and our meat hangs upon our bodies, as though it had been masticated by every mouth. A night comes when man weeps and woman is emptied.

She had finally come to fling herself down in this boy's room, with the feeling that she was about to die, and that she must die in the most presentable place. And here, prostrate on his chair, she was a stricken beast, with one last breath stirring in its frame, who breathed it out once and for evermore, and still looked lingeringly at its lair, before laying down its carcass.

Then she said:

'Let me sleep here, I can't go out. I ask you this because I know it's going to cause you a lot of bother.'

Thus spoke a harlot whose nights were as precious to her as a trade, who reckoned each of them at ten francs, and for whom a night lost was a day without bread. She asked a favour, she who knew the cost of favours, and knew as well that a human body has its price, and that you receive money from those you relieve.

He lay down beside her. He took her in his arms where she was cold, from head to foot, like an icy tempest, like a stony field where the harvest has been destroyed. He took her to his heart and kept her warm there for a long time with his burning devotion, a small lament of pity that came forth like a flame. He did not say a word, he did not think of the woman, but enveloped himself in this grief, and he felt like crying out:

'Poor little saint, poor little saint!'

CHAPTER IX

DECEMBER and the first of January came and went; but since Blanche's departure, the days passed wearily, as though time itself lacked enthusiasm.

One afternoon, at four o'clock, Berthe was passing the church of Saint-Leu on the Boulevard Sébastopol. It was a church of grey, rugged stone, like the buildings around the Halles, which reminded you of the fish-market and the heavy jaws of the fish-wives. For some days past, Berthe had felt a sort of breathlessness in her, a bodily distress from diaphragm to heart, whose significance she did not as yet suspect. At times she had strange ideas which began but came to nothing, and yet left in her a sort of gentleness and flavour. As she passed in front of the church of Saint-Leu, this breathless gasp gasped in her and took full possession of her. She smiled as she followed the impulse, saying to herself: 'Let's go in!'

She entered and walked twice around the church in amazement. Then she sat down on a chair, and, for a moment, she did not know what to say:

'Dear God, I am only a poor tramp. I wanted to come into the church of Saint-Leu tonight, without knowing why. Because I'm in Your Church, dear God, I think of You. You hardly look at us, because we do everything You have told us not to do. Maurice used to say: "There isn't any," but I, I tell You, there's a good God. It seems to me like I left the Boulevard Sébastopol a long time ago. Because I was sick the day of my first communion, I took my first communion two weeks later. We were two little girls in white from the same school: the holy sister took a cab and took us to Notre-Dame for our first communion. We were so happy to be in a cab. And then, I was the one my mother loved the best. She said to me: "Come here, Berthe, so I can curl your hair and make it nice." I went to catechism, and I'm still very fond of the Month of Mary. My mother was very good, she was not like other women, and she was an Italian. The day she died, I was in the hospital. My two sisters came to see me: Marthe was very white, but Blanche scratched her head and didn't seem much troubled by it. At the time, it didn't hurt me as much as I had thought. Dear God, I am thinking of my mother! I'd be so happy if I could see her again, but I wonder if all this I'm saying is not just nonsense. I'll pray to You, Father, because praying will make me feel better. If the people who know me knew I was praying, they'd think I was ridiculous, but I'll pray all the same. I'm only a street-girl, but I'm not wicked yet. You'll look at me, and You'll say: "Look, it's little Berthe Méténier saying her prayers!"'

She kneeled down and recited Our Father and Ave Maria, but though she tried hard she could not remember: I believe in God. A little later, she arose and sat down, and remained sitting in her corner, all alone and very quiet, like a little child who wants to set a good example.

She went out, and went straight to Pierre Hardy. She said to him:

'You can't imagine what I did this afternoon! I was passing by the church of Saint-Leu. I went in and I prayed to God for my mother's soul.'

There was in him a remainder of his Catholic education.

'Because of that, my little Berthe, many things will be forgiven you.'

Later, he realized that these words meant nothing.

After dinner, at the café, she said this: 'After all, I'm a fool to get all worked up.'

Then, seizing the bottle of alcohol, she poured its contents into her cup, with a gesture of determination and her head strangely throbbing. Truly, all sorts of queer ideas drove her, whirling together, and visible in her eyes as they passed. She began to laugh: 'Yes, sometimes it takes me like this!' She tossed off the alcohol as though it were water, and she wanted more.

She said: 'On with the dance!' She poured out more and more. The madness took her, and she tossed off a drink, tossed off another, a madness that leapt from hand to head, for drink was a joy that multiplied joy. She poured it down, as though drenching the soil, a gesture that set her off, which made her grow, and mingled in her sap an unknown force. She poured and poured, and it seemed as though she were pouring it down upon some actual thing.

At the street corner, there was a little urchin. Berthe, three-quarters dancing, swayed like a tight-rope dancer. She kicked her leg over the boy's head, saying: 'Whoops!' The child laughed. Berthe leaned over to kiss him and said: 'Isn't he sweet!'

For a moment the whole world seemed sweet. She put her energy into everything she saw, she embellished things with an enthusiasm of her own, and willingly would have swung them with her in the whirlpool.

> Mignonne, c'est la garde
> Qui passe en ce moment,
> Pan ran pan pan pan pan,

she sang, and she rushed into the open doorway of a café.

'I don't give a damn, I don't give a damn! It's been going on long enough. I'm fed up with all this fuss. You spit in the air and it falls on your nose. I don't give a damn now, and it's much better. There are people who say to me: "Lucky

you're good-natured, you're always laughing!" To hell
with them! I want a good time now. Oh, I know I had a
nervous fit tonight, but where did that get me, I'd like to
know? It's not worry that puts money in your pocket. Hey,
look at the old crone over there! He slobbers all over when
he drinks his beer. Looks like his beard was full of worms.
They're all right, old men. You say to them: "Give me two
francs extra and I'll kiss you." What must Maurice be
getting in the neck there in jail? A week now he's been
expecting to hear from me! Well, I was fed up. Funny how
you see people's faults when they're at a distance! What
d'you think his pal had the nerve to say to me the other day?
"It's not right," he said, "what you're doing now." Why
the devil can't he mind his own business, the fool?'

But Pierre, seated and very straight, opened his mouth,
and immediately she was quiet. There was something else in
the air.

'No, he who is your man is a man, and all flesh, the flesh
that suffers and the soul that labours, should be dearer to our
hearts than every desire and every hatred and should abide
there like a cry which howls until we offer it our love. I
know that a man has done you harm, but above all I know
that this man has been chastised and that this man is alone.
If your pain is great, act so that it is beautiful, bow your
head like a good angel beneath the Justice of God, then raise
your head and smile at your brother Satan. He brought you
light when you were seventeen, he sat for you in the morning, and as he took your hands he said: "Sister of my soul,
have you any understanding of my love?" Berthe and
Maurice, when the days entangled you, a miracle of the
Holy Ghost was then enacted, and it binds you today, and
should mark for evermore in your memory the instant of
Happiness that has passed. Today, they have driven this man
away. And I tell you: you must forget this man because he

has poured the abomination of the males upon your head, but I kneel at your feet and I beseech you, if that man be wounded, go and staunch his blood. Say to him: "I think of you who are in the pit of hell, and I send you my breath to cool the flames." And because there will be a day of resurrection, because the torments are not everlasting, on that day you will raise your brow, and you will answer: "I was a sister of charity, and I dressed your wounds. I am a woman whom you wounded, and who wishes to live. If you are healed, I am a woman who wishes to live, and to be healed, and who no longer knows you."'

This is not how Pierre spoke, this is not how Berthe heard him speak, but these words dominated the atmosphere around their heads and passed over them like a breath above their human words.

She asked for pen and paper, and as she wrote, it was with all the madness of a prostitute and a deceitful woman. She called him 'my dear little man,' and she wrote: 'I am weeping as I write these words,' and laughed because she was writing thus. She was wheedling in the Parisian way, whereby a smile is worn for the people met in the street, and whereby everything is carried off with French irony.

Again she started drinking down glasses of a stiff *marc* which she swallowed at one gulp, and called by an endearing name: a little *marc*. They followed one after the other in Indian file like children playing: she took them and shoved them deep into her guts, in a rage to smother what might still be there. When she was drunk, her drunkenness went through her entire body, ran through her nerves and made her laugh with a laughter that shook her and vibrated like a tightened spring. The whole world was funny, the match-containers on the tables, the gas-jets, the drinkers and the benches looked at her with an unfamiliar air that made her gesticulate and bubble over with laughter.

At last, they left. The street was black with thaw, the stars riddled the atmosphere and came down like hail, the noise of the traffic thundered by, and Berthe in her lucid and jerky drunkenness said:

'I don't know what's eating me, but I was never so sad as tonight.'

He took her home, and the moment they came in, the crisis broke. The landlady of the hotel was waiting for them:

'Mademoiselle, your brother passed by to see you. Here's the note he left.'

She read it and understood all her presentiments:

Her father had just died.

Jean Méténier died in the hospital at the age of forty-nine. One night, heavy as a stone, he went to bed, and during four days he writhed with painter's colic. Then he clenched his fists, stretched out on his back and felt the weight of his seven children on his skull: Marthe with her two brats, Berthe with Bubu, Blanche at Saint-Lazare with all the scum, Gustave living with big Marie who often loafed, and the three little kids who ate so much bread and who were there with their sparrow-like bills open— he died, his teeth clenched, and his jaw thrust forward.

It was during those days that Berthe was so unhappy. We always hope to see them again, and say: 'I made a mistake, but I loved you all the same. I will come home and now the family will be complete.' He was dead, and Berthe remembered, above all, something Gustave had told her. One day, their father had come upon Blanche in the rue de la Gaîté, hanging on the arm of a pimp. He came home, put his head in his hands and said: 'I had three daughters, they would have to be three sluts.' And large manly tears had fallen into his beard. He was dead, and this was an irreparable and unexpected thing. There was little filial sentiment left in her, and yet, when she looked upon the just and grave countenance of the dead, it was as though she were lashed by an eternal reproach. She was frightened as one is frightened in sleep by nightmares, by remorse, when the obscurity is thick and weighs, after the crime, like a punishment. She was ashamed because of the past, saw it suddenly in its entirety as in a vision before her eyes, and thought: 'I am the lowest of the low.'

And then she needed mourning clothes. That night, she made some excuse to leave the others, and she went out to earn her mourning dress. As usual, she did the Boulevard Sébastopol. She walked three hours, her feet on the stones, in the dreadful air of a night of death, and at the end, it seemed to her she was dragging the corpse along the street. She made two men. The first gave her ten francs, and, when she was lying on the bed, Berthe, the mechanical and passive harlot, found joy in the male and felt some pleasure in love. The second gave her five francs, and bargained. Never would she be able to forget that man. He had a red beard, and she wanted to bite him and say: 'But aren't you ashamed of rolling around on top of me the day I've lost my father!'

That night was her salvation. When shame is so strong that you can bear it no longer, you sit down, still blushing, but you look elsewhere, you go far from shame, and this must be. She had that taste in her mouth during those days, so long when we have lost our father: a taste of stone and ashes, of the Boulevard Sébastopol, and of the hospital where we die. And all her trade was full of it, all her days of pox and of infamy and of hotel rooms, where you lie down upon a bed, like a beast bereft of consciousness and bereft of thought. She saw again unnameable objects, basins and clothes flung on the floor, and the drained body of a whore on nights of work. She remembered it all: the long tramp on the boulevards, drinks in cafés, the tasteless kisses, all this mixed and melted into a single mass, and in her memory all these nights became the night when her father was to be buried.

There was a family reunion. The grandmother, like an old Carabosse fairy, looked at her with sharp eyes. She said:

'You dung-heap!'

Berthe replied:

'I don't know what you did when you were young!'

Her brother said:

'You keep quiet.'

They had disposed of the three little kids: Marthe was to take the second, Gustave the two others. All this had been settled before her face, without consulting her, without letting her speak, as though she were not one of the family. When she suggested coming to their help now and then, Gustave made an impatient gesture, as though to say: look after yourself first!

In the midst of all this, she shrivelled, in the undefinable anguish of the banished, and in a sort of terror that made her a little tremulous. She felt she was not respectable and, as she stood there in the group around the dead man, she understood that to be respectable is a fine thing. Then she thought of pimps and orgies. The relentless affiliation of infamy and misfortune brought her to the blackest depths of despair, to a lost and yawning pit whose bitter waters filled her breast. Life formed an image in her awkward mind: she saw before her eyes two fragile shoulders menaced by great blows. She had a feeling of pity for herself, and to her lips came childish words: 'Poor littl' Berthe!'

Then she saw noble feelings dawn like the rising of the sun. She was illuminated, Mary Magdalene, and when she stood up to dry her wet face, it seemed to her that her heart was lit with the primal light. She glimpsed a well of love beyond all things, a great kindliness that soared on high, and whose softly moving wings fluttered upon her brow. She perceived all this without fully grasping it, but her soul was refreshed as after eating fruit. Alleluiah, the angels sang! There was on earth a perfume like the Month of Mary. When she thought of Pierre, she thought of her parents, of artificial flowers, and of the certainty of living calm and equable days. Oh, how she longed to sit down and watch time pass, without making a gesture, and with every idea flowing away with time!

'All the same, if anyone had predicted this last week, I wouldn't have believed it, because misfortune has been after me so long. I would have said: "Stop fooling! Once you've got to the state I'm in, you know very well that it's for always. And then it's impossible to do otherwise."' But she was already thinking that on Sunday she would go to the country and pick some flowers. When you leave the hospital, almost cured, they say you are bleached. She was bleached!

She thought: 'Of course, I won't make so much money, and it will be hard, because money is happiness. I won't have ten-franc days like on the Sébastopol, but whenever I think of it, the Boulevard makes me sick. No doubt, it's because I'm not so strong as my sister Blanche. And then, I didn't make the most of it. I don't know what gets into your blood when you do that trade. It's quite true that money made in a bad way does nobody any good. It seems to me that working in flowers, I'll have some quiet. I'll be busy all day, and so I won't want to spend so much money. And then, if you're good, you're always rewarded. I'll be sure to find someone who'll take an interest in my fate and be willing to help me out. Really, I think I'll stay good.

H

I don't care about making a home, because every man has his drawbacks.'

She went to look over the advertisements in the rue Réaumur and found work at once. It all happened as in the story-books where the sun nurses the convalescent back to health. Winter seemed to turn to spring, and in the sky there were patches of blue that vibrated in the sun, stretched over the roofs, and made you think of young loving couples. In the street, passers-by walked on the sunny side. She was fresh and lively and kind, with so wide a kindliness that it was easy to imagine that all the good weather issued from her heart. She worked in a gloomy workshop where old remnants of winter stagnated in the corners; the ill-tempered boss, and all the girls, with their idiotic jokes about love, at first seemed to her evil things, as she had seen in other days, at the awkward age. This was because she had lost the habit, but in a week she would be used to it all again.

When she left in the evening, she sought out Pierre. She told him the news: 'You understand, I was fed up.

'Here's what I'll do: I'll take a small room for five francs a week—no more. I'll settle down in this quarter. You'll see, my dear Pierre, sooner or later, this will finish in a wedding. Every evening, if you like, we'll take a walk in the rue de Rivoli, and then go home, each to his own room. From time to time, I'll go back with you to your room, but not every day, because we mustn't get too tired. But first, you must give me hospitality until I've got my first week's pay. You'll take me out to the restaurant. I won't make you spend much money. We're going to have a good time. We'll have a house-warming. I'll buy a chicken and have it roasted somewhere, and I'll get some vegetables and we'll have a nice little dinner. I want to get hold of a *filtre* to make coffee. You'll see, I'll make you a fine stew.'

And Pierre thought:

'I had no woman. I walked with bowed head saying to myself: "I have no woman." There is a continuity in misfortune that makes us believe that life is evil. But it's all over. I feel now that all I lacked is going to come to me, and that everything is as it should be. But equilibrium doesn't come at the first try. I keep asking myself: what have I done, what is my special merit, that so much happiness is given me?'

CHAPTER X

So Pierre and Berthe were sleeping, back to back, at three o'clock in the morning, on a night when desire had been spent. He felt her beside him like the calm breath of a tranquil life, like the certainty of a contentment that no longer moves us. She had fallen asleep because she was weary, and this weariness was like the weariness of a little child. It is the presence of a woman at night which seems to pause upon our brows, and which is lovelier than in the day, and which is far more penetrating. Oh, to sleep like this when it is happiness that sends us off to sleep, and folds about our slumber like some fine wool woven by pious hands! The woman is virgin and like our guardian angel.

When the three of them had reached the landing, Bubu pressed his ear to the door. He heard nothing, but it seemed to him he heard his arteries pound. In the darkness, Grand Jules touched Adèle:

'Go along.'

She knocked three times, then, with her fluty voice:

'Is Berthe there?'

They heard something; presently the door opened, and the light was lit.

Adèle walked in and said:

'You cause me such trouble.'

Then Bubu, in silence, removing his hat; then Grand Jules, with his cap on his head, very straight, closing the door. They were unexpected visitors.

Bubu, short and broad, took two strong steps, like a furniture-mover:

'Monsieur, I regret the circumstances. When a man's been four years with a woman, it costs something, you understand. I'm performing a duty.'

They both sat up in bed, with their shirts and shoulders, beside the quivering candle, and stared at it all, their eyes scorched by the sight of so many things. She felt a blow, all the slaps she had ever received, in a single blow. Bubu said:

'Get up, Madame.'

She sat up in bed with her narrow face, her senses halted, so weak that she no longer knew how to speak.

He repeated:

'Get up.'

As she did not move, Bubu realized that he who is right, must show his might. He stepped forward:

'Pardon me, Monsieur.'

And he slapped her soundly to bring her back to her duty.

Pierre started to say:

'But Monsieur, if you have claims . . .'

Grand Jules cut him short:

'Yes, we have claims.'

And to Berthe, who was getting up, Grand Jules said:

'You're lucky, Madame, to have a man who loves you.'

Then he said:

'You know, we came here as friends. We didn't want to make trouble for you. I asked the clerk: "Where is Hardy's room? We're friends who have come to wake him up."'

And Bubu added:

'I beg you to excuse me, Monsieur, for calling on you at this hour of the night. I'll come back and see you, to make my excuses, so you'll see me in a better light.'

And here Adèle felt faint, and her fine trick upset her and made her cry. Berthe had said to her :'I know a kind young man who's called so-and-so . . .'

And Adèle had told everything to the other.

Bubu took her hand.

'Are you tired, my child?'

Pierre had some tea on the table, and Bubu started to pour some out into a glass.

Then he changed his mind:

'I must wash the glass. You must take precautions with Madame. Madame has the pox. Madame has sores in her mouth.'

Berthe was dressing, and her clothes slipped over her like the silence of night, when a ghost looks and stretches his shadowy limbs. She drew on her stockings, with holes at the heels, put on her garters, and it seemed to her that she was at the same time putting upon her body something infinitely sad. Then she put on her petticoat, and said:

'How was I to know you had got out?'

Bubu replied:

'That's all right, Madame. After having shown interest in a man as you have done, it would be surprising if you did not know that! So you didn't know I had got out? There is a thing called "probation", which you scarcely expected.'

She was very poorly clad for the cold of winter, and when she had put on her white jersey, there was nothing left to put on but her skirt and blouse. She combed her hair. She brought her black hair over her shoulder and combed it slowly, because she had plenty of time to see what was going to happen. Bubu said:

'So you still have some hair left! Hurry up, my beauty, we're in Monsieur's room and we mustn't wear out his patience.'

The first thought she had was of death. He was taking her away like an object that belonged to his life, one which he came to take from where it had been pawned. She felt herself a thing, a poor Berthe, shapeless and ill, who needed to sleep forever to forget . . . If I refused to follow him, he would kill me . . . She preferred to reflect a little before death, and owe it only to her own desire. Now she took up her blouse and skirt.

Grand Jules said:

'You see, Monsieur, that we have acted like friends. We know who you are and that Madame has only told you what she felt inclined to. Permit me to roll a cigarette before I go downstairs, and to shake hands with you.'

Bubu said:

'I regret, Monsieur, to have caused you all this disturbance. It was very kind of you to take Madame in as you did. Permit me to come and see you soon and offer you a drink. I shake your hand, but believe me, it is a very painful duty that I have performed.'

They went out. On the landing, Bubu asked:

'Did you get paid for your night of love, Madame?'

She came back.

'They want you to give me some money.'

'Here's five francs.'

She went into a world where individual benevolence has no power, because there is love and money, and because those who wreak evil are implacable and because prostitutes carry the brand of it from the start like passive animals that are led to the common pasture.

The downstairs door banged. Pierre already understood:

'Oh, I know that you will weep! My God, but I have no luck! You haven't courage enough to deserve happiness. Weep and die! Even though you were alone, you should have gone down in your shirt and your bare feet and cried out: "Help!" You should have gone down into the street and clutched hold of the passers-by, and cried: "Come quickly. They're murdering a woman up there!"'